Most Likely to Die
(A Miranda and Parker Mystery) Book 16

Linsey Lanier

Proofread by

Donna Rich

Copyright © 2019 Linsey Lanier
Felicity Books
All rights reserved.

ISBN: 1-941191-62-2
ISBN-13: 978-1-941191-62-0

Copyright © 2019 Linsey Lanier

All rights reserved. Without limiting the rights under copyright reserved above, no part of this publication may be reproduced, stored in or introduced into a retrieval system, or transmitted, in any form, or by any means (electronic, mechanical, photocopying, recording, or otherwise) without the prior written permission of both the copyright owner and the above publisher of this book. This is a work of fiction. Names, characters, places, brands, media, and incidents are either the product of the author's imagination or are used fictitiously. The author acknowledges the trademarked status and trademark owners of various products referenced in this work of fiction, which have been used without permission. The publication/use of these trademarks is not authorized, associated with, or sponsored by the trademark owners.

MOST LIKELY TO DIE

Just a few weeks ago, PI Miranda Steele thought
the love of her life was dead.

Parker believed the same about her.

Miraculously, they made it through the worst ordeal of their lives, and have
retired to the peace and quiet of the North Georgia Mountains.

But it's a little too peaceful here, and Miranda is getting restless.

As a diversion they decide to attend a high school reunion party in Chicago.
Nothing dangerous about that, right?

But when a former classmate is found dead, Miranda and Parker are pulled
out of retirement to investigate what could be a bizarre murder.
Not exactly what they had planned.

And things are about to turn deadly.

This time, they might not survive.

THE MIRANDA'S RIGHTS MYSTERY SERIES

Someone Else's Daughter
Delicious Torment
Forever Mine
Fire Dancer
Thin Ice

THE MIRANDA AND PARKER MYSTERY SERIES

All Eyes on Me
Heart Wounds
Clowns and Cowboys
The Watcher
Zero Dark Chocolate
Trial by Fire
Smoke Screen
The Boy
Snakebit
Mind Bender
Roses from My Killer
The Stolen Girl
Vanishing Act
Predator
Retribution
Most Likely to Die
(more to come)

MAGGIE DELANEY POLICE THRILLER SERIES

Chicago Cop
Good Cop Bad Cop

OTHER BOOKS BY LINSEY LANIER

Steal My Heart

For more information visit www.linseylanier.com

CHAPTER ONE

This was going to be the best night of her life. Or at least one of them.

Turning this way and that, she carefully checked herself over in the full length mirror in the hotel's elegant marble bathroom.

She smiled at her reflection.

Her hair was perfect, cut to just the right length and falling over her shoulders in the way that always made men swoon. Her makeup was just right, too. She'd used that new eye shadow method she'd found on YouTube recently.

And the nightgown? Well.

The black Victoria's Secret special in scalloped eyelash lace hugged her curves as if she'd been poured into it. And its dramatic plunge down the front showed off her best feature in a way that would have him eating out of the palm of her hand the second he arrived.

She knew her assets. And how to use them to get what she wanted.

Lipstick. She could do with a bit more.

She grabbed the tube, drew it over her lips, smacked them together.

Perfect.

With a squeal of excitement, she put the tube away and danced into the bedroom, the fabric of her negligee flowing behind her like a regal robe.

She eyed the clean sweeping lines of the light colored furnishings and the pretty blue and white carpet. It wasn't the suite she'd asked for. It was just a room with a king size bed. But it was nice. And in one of the best hotels in Chicago, in fact.

She wasn't going to let him put her in some fleabag motel. Not with the kind of money he had.

She went to the table near the window and touched the champagne bottle chilling on ice in its decanter. The two flutes beside it reflected the lights from the magnificent view of the city below. They were going to have fun tonight.

She looked at the clock. He'd be here any minute.

Her heart beating in anticipation, she went to the door, unlatched it, and left it ajar. That would make him feel welcome and spike his curiosity at the same time. She wasn't worried about anyone unwanted busting in on her. She had her little snub-nose eight shot revolver in the nightstand, and she knew how to use it.

It was legal and all. She had the proper ID and license for concealed carry.

She knew how to take care of herself.

Crossing to the bed, she lay down on the thick satiny duvet. Resting an arm on one of the embossed pillows, she struck a pose she knew would make his brows rise—and something else, as well.

She sighed happily.

No, this wasn't about money. And it wasn't going to be a one-night fling. This was more. She hadn't thought she could feel this way again. All tingly and giddy and schoolgirlish. Not after all these years and so much water under the bridge.

But she did.

Tonight would be the start of something new. Something life altering.

She looked at the clock again and scowled. He was late.

He used to pride himself on being punctual. Oh, well. Some things were worth waiting for, weren't they? She closed her eyes and imagined how she'd feel in his arms again.

Minutes passed. An hour. Another hour. And another.

At one a.m., she got up and checked on the champagne. The ice was melted, the bottle's contents were probably near room temperature.

She didn't care. She popped it open, poured some into one of the flutes, and swallowed a big mouthful.

She stomped over to the door, anger burning inside her. Nobody stood her up. Nobody humiliated her like this.

But he had. And it wasn't the first time.

Gritting her teeth, she turned the lock and went back to the bed. At least she'd have a night in a nice hotel room.

Then she opened the drawer of the nightstand and stared down at her snub-nose revolver. Nobody did this to her. Nobody got away with something like this.

She'd make him pay.

She took out the gun, released the cylinder, and checked the bullets. All eight were there. She snapped it shut and blinked back the tears that were starting to come.

She knew what she had to do. It was clear as day. Simple.

She had to kill him.

CHAPTER TWO

Miranda Steele stood on the strip of red clay that sloped around the North Georgia Mountain cabin and led into the tall pine forest. With the warm April breeze caressing her face and outdoor smells all around her, she stretched out her hand.

Before her a young white-tailed doe stood, ears alert, nostrils twitching. Slowly the animal eased toward her open palm.

Then, with the speed of a sniper bullet, the doe snatched the slice of apple Miranda had been holding and scurried off into the woods.

"Hey, there's more."

But the doe was gone.

Miranda sighed with sympathy. She knew what it was like to have trust issues. The doe would not return soon.

Instead of waiting, she bent to put the rest of the apple down on the path, then turned and headed back around the rear of the cabin.

Cabin. It was more like a luxury resort hidden in the mountain woods. A sprawling two-story structure of red cedar, it featured three roomy bedrooms, a huge kitchen and dining room, an even bigger living room, and a wrap-around porch.

It was nice. Really nice. Her whole life now was nice.

Even if it was a little dull.

As she rounded the far corner, she looked up and caught sight of the handsome figure standing on the porch grinning at her.

Her heart swelled with joy.

Now that was the reason she was here. Wade Russell Parker the Third. Former President and CEO of the Parker Investigative Agency.

And he wasn't dull in the least bit.

He was alive.

Alive. Not shot dead by a vicious criminal. Alive. Not floating at the bottom of some ocean. Alive. She still had a profound sense of relief every time she saw him.

Dressed in casual designer jeans and a blue polo shirt that set off both the gray of his eyes and his dark neatly styled hair with the salt-and-pepper touches at the temples, he looked strong and fit again.

Dr. Taggart had insisted on realigning his nose, and except for a little bruising under the eyes that was going away nicely, he was as heart-stoppingly handsome as ever.

And even more muscular. He'd filled one of the extra rooms in the cabin with a gym-full of exercise equipment and had been working out every day to regain his strength.

Miranda knew losing it was a sore spot for him.

"Breakfast is ready," he called, drinking her in with his gaze.

He was just as glad to see her alive every morning as she was to see him. He'd thought she was dead, too.

"Is it?" She began to climb the red cedar stairs to where he was standing.

"Now that you've fed all the wildlife in the woods you can think of feeding yourself."

She smirked. "It was just one doe. She looked hungry."

"Not as hungry as I am." He took her hand and kissed her as she reached him.

He wasn't talking about food.

He pulled her close and murmured against her cheek. "I could stand out here all day with you if breakfast wouldn't get cold."

"Well, we can't have that." With a laugh, she pulled away, gave him a peck on the cheek, and let him lead her through the door.

Inside she was greeted by the familiar solid paneled walls of Western cedar, rustic tables, and comfy overstuffed sofas in soft blue checkered fabrics. The place was as homey and woodsy as a fairytale.

She took a deep breath and her mouth watered at the familiar aroma in the air. "Hmm. Coffee."

"Of course." As Parker guided her into the dining room and seated her in one of the farmhouse driftwood chairs, the smells grew more intense and delicious.

On the large raw wood table under cheery blue placemats sat two country style plates laden with huge omelets.

"You outdid yourself this morning," she grinned, picking up the napkin that matched the placemat.

She lifted the big mug of black liquid beside the plate to her lips, took a sip, and let out a moan of pleasure. She'd never get tired of Parker's fancy imported coffee.

After he'd learned she had given all of his away to Estavez when she thought she'd never see her husband again, he'd bought a whole case and taken it with them to the mountains.

She was glad he had.

Lifting her fork, she dug into the omelet and took a bite. She had to moan again as her tongue was caressed by onions, peppers, imported Swiss cheese, and oh! Extra hot jalapenos.

"Yum!" she said with her mouth still full.

Grinning with pleasure, Parker sat down beside her and reached for his napkin. "I'm glad you're pleased."

"Your cooking skills have improved."

"A few videos provided the necessary information."

Plus he knew what she liked. Savoring the pampering as much as the omelette, she dove into the scrumptious fare.

As Parker watched her relishing the food he had prepared, he was filled with a special kind of delight he hadn't known before he thought he had lost her forever.

He had always loved her. From the first moment he'd gazed into those expressive deep blue eyes with their sharp black lashes. From the first day she'd walked into his office and let him know she was no pushover. From their first sparring session in the Agency gym when he'd first tasted her. But now, his love was richer, deeper than he could ever have imagined.

It filled him with impossible joy.

His lovely wife was alive and with him in one of his favorite spots on earth. He couldn't be happier.

But he knew her.

He knew her talents, her strengths, her instincts, her sharp mind. And he knew she was growing just a bit restless up here in the mountains.

He would have to keep her occupied. It would be his new career after retiring from the Agency. They could not go back to investigative work. They would not. They had promised each other. Never again would he risk her life. Never again would he risk his own.

No matter what.

Although there was the side project he'd been working on. But that was an exception. He studied the nuances in Miranda's face closely to make sure she hadn't seen the laptop across the room that he'd shut down before he'd gone out to the porch.

There was nothing obvious in her expression, but she had learned how to hide her feelings. Even at times from him.

But he couldn't let himself think of their past or the future. They had to learn to live in the moment.

Right now, watching her enjoy the meal he'd prepared was enough. They would both have to be content with the little things.

He picked up his coffee cup and took a sip. "What would you like to do today?"

Miranda swallowed the last bite of omelet and checked her gaze before it landed on Parker's laptop across the room.

The one with its lid closed that she'd spotted when she'd come inside.

Cooking videos, huh? She knew what he'd been doing. Checking obscure news stories, digging into secret sites with tidbits on FBI activity. Scanning police calls along the Gulf of Mexico. All in the hope he could find out what had happened to Donovan Santana.

She knew because she'd been doing the same thing.

So far, she'd come up with nothing, and she was pretty sure Parker hadn't, either. There was no sign of the man or the boat he'd escaped in. She could only hope Simon Sloan was organizing some kind of secret search party and would have Santana in custody soon. With the way Sloan operated, they might never even know about it.

Maybe that was for the best.

Sipping her coffee, she gazed out at the gorgeous blue-green mountains through the huge picture window. As beautiful as this place was, as happy as she was to be here with Parker, she was getting a little tired of tourist activities.

"We could go to the museum," Parker suggested.

She wrinkled her nose. "We did that yesterday."

"River rafting?"

"We did that last week."

"We could go hiking and see the waterfalls."

"We did that two days ago."

"Hmm." Parker set down his cup. "Explore the town and find a new restaurant?"

She scowled. "We just ate."

The truth was she was bored. And they'd only been here a week.

The disappointment on his face stinging her, she got up and took her dishes to the kitchen. "We'll think of something fun to do."

Carrying his own plate, Parker followed her.

As she turned on the water and reached for the soap, he leaned in and began to nibble her neck. "I can think of several fun things."

They'd just done that, too. But making love to Parker was something she'd never get tired of. Just now, the tickling sensations he was sending across her shoulders were irresistible.

She barely got the water turned off when he began inching her toward the bedroom.

"My hands are still wet," she laughed.

"All the better for what I have in mind."

His lips moved to hers as he turned her and began edging her backward across the wooden floor, through the hall, into the bedroom, and toward the big four poster bed.

When she felt the flowery red spread with the back of her leg, she sank back onto the cushy mattress and pulled him to her, drinking in his heady kisses like a survivalist on a reality show craving water.

Without breaking the kiss, she scooted up to the pillows. He moved with her, his hands pulling at her shirt, stroking her sides, making her flesh quiver.

Then his lips were against her cheek again. "If you don't want to stay here," he murmured, "we could take a trip,"

It took her a minute to realize he was still talking about how to occupy their time. Other than with the present activity.

She broke the kiss and blinked at him. Maybe he could multitask like that, but she couldn't.

She fluffed a pillow and stuck it under her head. "A trip? To where?"

His gaze drank her in, letting her know he wasn't nearly finished with her. "Anywhere you'd like. Somewhere in Europe, perhaps."

She had to think a moment. It was true. They didn't have to stay in the mountains. They could go anywhere in the world. And not for work. For pleasure. All kinds of pleasure.

"Not Paris," she said. She could still feel the reverberation under her feet from the ordeal they'd gone through there.

"London? We could see Mackenzie."

She pursed her lips. "Not sure how Colby and Oliver would feel about that." Besides Mackenzie had texted her that school was really hard over there and she was always studying.

"Maui? To see your father?" He inched up beside her and once more ran his hand over her body, making her shiver.

Giving in, she pulled his mouth to hers again. Right now she was getting ready for a trip to the stars.

Suddenly a loud piercing laugh shot through the air.

They both jumped up as if they'd been caught stealing the crown jewels.

"What the heck is that?" Miranda asked, her heart pounding.

Parker scowled. "My cell phone. I thought you weren't going to put any more prank ringtones on it."

Oh, yeah. She lifted her palms. "Force of habit." She would have to stop doing that. It always backfired on her.

Parker sat up and looked at the display.

Miranda pouted at the cell-us interruptus. "What is it?"

"An email from Cybil."

She raised a brow. "Cybil at the Agency?"

"I told her to contact me if she had any questions."

Since Parker had come back from the dead, Miranda had lost her head honcho status at the Agency. Not that she cared about it. But Holloway was supposed to be running things now.

"She's asking about an email sent to you."

"Me?" Miranda tensed.

"Do you know anyone named Jane Anderson?"

"Jane Anderson." Her mind drew a blank. "Never heard of her."

The corner of Parker's mouth turned up. "It's an invitation to your high school reunion."

"My what?" She sat up and took the phone from him. "Oh. That Jane Anderson."

The one she hadn't thought about since—since she'd used her name in a lie the first time she went to Mockingbird Hills.

But she smiled as she read the text.

Miranda,

I'm sorry this is such short notice, but I just figured out how to contact you. I hope you can come.

We're going to have a great time.

Jane

P.S: We're doing a Nineteen Year Reunion instead of a Twenty because I'll be in Europe next year.

The attached invitation was full of fancy fonts and digital sparkles. The theme was going to be Prom Night.

Miranda had to smile. Her high school reunion. She never thought she'd be invited to one.

She held up the phone. "This might be fun."

Parker didn't seem impressed. "Are you sure you want to go back to Chicago, Miranda? And see people you knew in high school?"

She knew what he meant.

That was when she met Leon and began her descent into hell. And in fact, she hadn't even finished high school.

But she hadn't had a nightmare in weeks. The living nightmare she and Parker had endured recently had upstaged all her bad dreams. That was why they were here in the North Georgia Mountains. Retired from chasing killers all over the globe.

"Miranda?"

She met his piercing gaze, then eyed the invitation again. "The theme is Prom Night. I never got to go to a prom."

He put a finger under her chin and turned her face toward him. "Do you want to go?"

She didn't know why, didn't know why Jane Anderson had thought of her after all this time, especially since she didn't graduate with the class.

But yeah, she did want to go.

Then she scrolled to the bottom of the screen and her shoulders sank. "We're too late. It's tonight."

Parker took the phone out of her hand and read the invitation. "It starts at eight p.m."

"It's in Chicago. At some fancy hotel downtown. We're here in the North Georgia Mountains."

"There is such a thing as a jet plane."

And Parker was just the type to drop a load on plane tickets just to please her. "Do you really think we could make it?"

"Of course, we can. So you see? We're not late at all." He kissed her hard as he turned her over and finally got her shirt over her head. "We even have time to finish what we started here."

CHAPTER THREE

Parker's timeline cut it close.

By four that afternoon, he and Miranda had taken a two-hour drive to Hartsfield-Jackson airport, a three-hour flight to O'Hare International Airport, and a fifty-minute drive into the city and through the tall skyscrapers in a shiny red Jaguar sports car Parker had rented.

Now she was standing before a mirror in a high-end dress shop on Chicago's Magnificent Mile in an off white floor-length dress she found drab and itchy.

Parker held up a hanger that held a shimmering gown. "Moonlight silver sequins instead?"

His taste always ran to glamorous.

She wrinkled her nose. "That's a bit much." She didn't want to stick out like a neon sign.

"I don't suppose this one will do."

From the nearby rack he lifted a flowing blush pink maxi with lots of flounce. It reminded her of the babydoll getup he'd selected the first time he took her dress shopping.

"Uh, no."

After another ten minutes of shuffling through the selections, they decided on a black Georgette crepe with a halter top, sheer shoulder straps, and a low back. She liked that the long sweeping skirt would hide her feet.

"I can wear my sneakers under this."

Parker's eyes narrowed. "We'll compromise with your low heel pumps."

"You'll owe me for that."

He grinned sexily. "I look forward to paying up."

But there wasn't time for making out now.

Next they were off to pick up a black tux for Parker, which was a whole lot easier than dress shopping. And then they were back in the car and headed down Michigan Avenue, through the honking traffic.

"Where to now?"

"The wisdom on the reunion blogs advises eating before you go," Parker said turning onto a side street.

"Won't they be serving food?" She thought she'd read something like that in the invitation.

"Appetizers," Parker said. "If you get to chatting with your old friends, you might not get a bite."

And they couldn't have that. Parker's mission since they'd gone to the mountains was to make sure she gained back the weight she had lost over the past weeks.

Miranda looked up and saw a wine-colored awning over a set of glass doors etched with gold lettering. On the walkway stood several men in uniforms. Valets.

One of them came around the car, opened her door, and took her hand to help her out. Parker got out, handed the keys to the Jaguar to another valet, and extended an arm to her.

Feeling like a queen, she tucked her hand in his arm and they stepped inside.

Soon they were seated in a rust-colored suede booth under low lights, taking in the sparkling glasses and large avant garde artwork on the walls.

A waiter came to take their orders.

The scent of chargrilled meat was tempting, but Parker stuck to his heart smart regimen and ordered Ahi Tuna with avocado and cucumber, while Miranda selected seared sea scallops with grilled squash and artichokes.

Everything was five-star scrumptious, and she was stuffed when they finished, much to Parker's satisfaction. Though she would have loved to linger over dessert, the clock was ticking.

Time to check in to their hotel and get changed.

Thoughtfully, Parker had booked a place a couple miles from the one they'd stayed in the last time they were in the city. And it was just a block or two from where the reunion would take place.

Of course, he got them a suite, with a view of the river, no less. Stepping inside, Miranda took in the modern style decor, the light colored upholstery, the richly textured dark purple accents, and the ebony furnishings.

It would do.

And, of course, there was a huge master bath featuring a deliciously marbled sunken tub—for later.

Parker would never stop spoiling her.

They showered and dressed quickly, and when Miranda stepped out of the bedroom in her gorgeous gown and got a load of her classy hubby, her heart swooned.

Tall and muscular in his black tux and bowtie with his expensive leather shoes, he reminded her of the night they met—in a Fulton County jail cell back in Atlanta.

Like that night, his dark salt-and-pepper hair was neatly combed, except for the stray wisps of his hair falling seductively over his forehead. The lines in his handsome face gave him a dark, sophisticated look that made James Bond look like a beach bum.

They stood there, staring at each other a long moment, his piercing gray eyes taking her in and sending chills through her.

Then she noticed what was in his silk lapel. A single white rose with a tasteful spray of baby's breath. A plastic container sat on the coffee table. There were flowers in it.

"Is that for me?"

"It is prom night, isn't it?" He reached down and handed it to her.

She opened it and found a purple orchid with a spray of white roses on a pearl band.

She started to tear up. "Oh, Parker."

"You do like it, don't you?"

"I love it." Blinking back her emotions she grinned at him. "Did I ever tell you you're the most thoughtful man in the world?"

"I aim to please." Beaming with pleasure, Parker took the fragrant flowers out of the box and slipped them over her wrist. "The perfect touch for that dress."

"I'll say." She did feel like a schoolgirl. "And there's nothing like a handsome man in a tux." She grinned as he swept her into his arms.

"And the beautiful woman at his side." He brushed her temple with his lips.

"Mmm. Maybe we should just have our own reunion right here."

"Are you changing your mind about going?"

She thought a moment. Suddenly a flock of butterflies began fluttering their wings in her stomach.

What the heck was that all about? She'd faced down vicious serial killers and other assorted criminals. She wasn't afraid of a bunch of high school kids.

Even if they were grown up now.

She grabbed her bag and headed for the door. "Not on your life, buddy. I'm ready to party."

With a knowing grin, he opened the door for her. "Let's be on our way, then."

CHAPTER FOUR

The reunion was being held at the Royal Rose Hotel, another classy five-star spot right down the street from the one Parker had booked them.

It had an Asian flare, and the lobby was all shimmering glass and elegant long stemmed flowers, both in pricey vases and stunning watercolors.

The party was in a banquet hall on the twentieth floor and featured what they called a rooftop terrace, though the main part of the hotel extended an additional twenty stories or so.

They rode up the elevator, crossed a golden hallway, and then on Parker's arm, Miranda stepped into the large reception room.

It was stunning.

High above, a circular ceiling with crystal chandeliers was draped in blue-and-gold banners. The school colors. From hidden projectors, old yearbook photos flashed across the high walls. Across the far wall, stretched another banner reading, "Welcome Baxter High School Alumni." An instrumental version of the school fight song played softly through speakers.

Chatting in small clusters, about seventy people stood near circular tables covered with blue-and-gold tablecloths set up along the edge of a dance floor. The men were in tuxedos and wore boutonnieres in their lapels. The women were in floor length gowns. Some wore dress gloves. Most were adorned with corsages or nosegays. The whole place smelled of flowers.

Looked like they'd fit right in. Except for their timing.

"We're late," she whispered to Parker.

"Fashionably so."

"Hello, are you here for the Baxter High reunion?"

Miranda turned to see a blond woman in a peach chiffon gown sitting at a greeting table. She tried hard to place her.

Nope. As far as she knew, she'd never seen this person in her life.

She cleared her throat. "Uh, yes. I got an email from Jane Anderson."

"Name?"

"Miranda Steele." She pointed her thumb at Parker. "This is my plus one."

"Hello there," said another blond woman sitting beside the first one at the table. She was in a pale green chiffon gown and looked a lot like the first woman. "Take a favor."

With a gloved hand, she gestured to a basket filled with silver mesh bags tied with blue-and-gold ribbons.

Miranda took one.

"Instructions are on the card."

"Card?"

Miranda opened her bag and found the card along with a post-it pad and a small pen.

She held the card out so Parker could read it.

Play the Most Likely To Game.

Start a conversation with someone by asking, "What have you been up to since graduation?"

Listen to the answer and try to guess what the person was voted Most Likely To in the year book.

Write your guess on the post-it note with the person's name and drop it in the bowl at the front.

Winners will be selected at the end of the party.

"An interesting ice breaker," Parker said.

"A memory test. And it ensures everyone stays until the end."

"Wait a minute." The woman at the table held up a clipboard, "I don't see your name on my list."

Miranda shifted her weight. This could be a very short night.

Then she turned and saw another woman staring at her from a few feet away.

Small and demure looking, her dress was an off white ivory with an elegant embossed pattern. Her medium brown hair was straight and cut just under her chin. The ash blond highlights gave her a classy sophisticated look.

Her large doe like brown eyes were open wide in astonishment. "Miranda Steele, is that you?"

Miranda was speechless. She didn't know her from Adam's housecat.

Parker came to her rescue. "Would you by any chance be Jane Anderson?"

"Why yes, I am."

How did he guess that?

Jane Anderson's eyes flashed even wider as she got a look at Parker, then she rushed over and gave Miranda a tight hug as if they were long lost friends.

In a way they were.

This was Jane Anderson? The girl Miranda remembered had stringy hair, glasses, and braces on her teeth.

"I didn't think you'd come."

Miranda laughed awkwardly. "A chance to see everyone I went to school with? How could I miss it?"

"It's been such a long time. We have so much to catch up on."

And then Miranda noticed someone else staring at her.

This one she did remember.

Tall and curvy, though she'd put on a little weight. She had the same thick, nearly black hair curling to her shoulders that Miranda had envied all those years ago. Her makeup was perfect, accentuating her piercing blue eyes. She was just as beautiful as back then. The most popular girl in school. Especially with the football team.

"Is that who I think it is?"

The woman let out a resonant squeal and hurried across the floor, the sleeves of her curve-hugging crimson dress fluttering. The gown's deep V-neck left little to the imagination.

Miranda forced a grin as she reached her. "La Stella, isn't it?"

"Stella La Stella," she said in an I'm-so-much-better-than-you tone.

Miranda had never liked the girl. She recalled she'd once TP'd her locker.

Stella began to wave her hands, her red fingernails glittering under the lights as she spoke in a rich sultry voice. "Actually, I was Stella La Stella-Williams for a while. Then I was Stella La Stella-Perry. That was when I was in Hollywood. And until two and a half years ago, I was Stella La Stella-Schimmelpfennig. Now I'm back to just plain Stella La Stella."

Three husbands. Interesting. But there was nothing plain about her. Miranda remembered her as Most Likely To...

Jane put a hand on the woman's arm. "Stella's our class celebrity. She's the weather girl on WTG."

"Weather person," Stella corrected. "And I'm a forecaster, though I'm taking meteorology courses online, and I'm filling in for the meteorologist who's on vacation next week. It's a fun gig and who knows where it could lead."

"Stella's my co-coordinator for the reunion," Jane said. "She's been a big help."

Stella La Stella and Jane Anderson? Hard to imagine those two as friends. Miranda recalled Stella knocking books out of Jane's arms in the hallway back in high school.

But time could do strange things to relationships.

Stella pointed at Miranda. "And what about you, Miranda Steele? I thought you married that guy who used to hang around on the corner at school."

She meant Leon. "I did."

"Did you? Gee, I thought he was a drug dealer."

"Actually he was a cop."

"Really? What happened? If you don't mind my asking."

Didn't mind at all. "I shot him."

Stella blinked. Then she laughed and shook her head. "Oh, Miranda. You always were such a hoot."

Was she?

Stella smiled at Parker, whom she'd been stealing glances at. "Where did you get this hunk?"

"I found him panhandling on Michigan Avenue and asked him if he wanted to go to a party tonight."

Stella's mouth opened in shock.

Waving off the remark, Jane laughed. "Oh, Miranda. Don't be silly. This is Wade Parker, Stella. He's a famous private investigator. Haven't you seen the news stories on TV?"

Jane had seen her and Parker on TV? Uh oh.

"Private investigator? Miranda Steele married a private investigator?"

"We're both private investigators," Parker explained, extending a hand. "I'm so happy to meet you, Ms. La Stella."

"Just Stella," she breathed, nearly drooling.

Parker's charm was really doing a number on her. But as she shook with him, her other hand went to her throat almost as she was afraid he was going to start interrogating her.

Miranda wondered what that was about.

Instead of asking, she thought about the instructions on that card.

She turned to Jane. "And what about you, Jane? What have you been up to during the past nineteen years?"

Jane pointed to Miranda's favor and smiled. "You're playing the game. Isn't it fun? It was Stella's idea."

Miranda wondered about that. She remembered Jane as the one who always kept track of things and put them in their place. She'd been class secretary their sophomore year. Miranda would put her down as Most Likely to Organize Her Closet.

"So what's your answer?"

"Me? Oh, I've kept busy. I went to Loyola for Paralegal Studies, got a job in a law firm, then I married Quinton Prescott. We have two boys. You remember Quinton, don't you?"

Another blank.

"He's over there."

Across the room near a glass wall shared with the terrace, two men were talking. The taller one was husky and broad shouldered. His dark blond hair sat on his head in tight waves. He wore a cobalt blue tux with a self-assured air, as if he'd purposely chosen the color to draw attention to himself. The white silk tie and pink rose in his lapel only added to the impression.

And yet with his hands in his pockets, he looked like he was sharing military secrets with the dark haired man next to him.

Now Miranda remembered him.

Quinton Prescott, captain of the football team. All star. Never missed the honor roll. Class President.

Most Likely to Succeed.

And Stella La Stella's steady boyfriend. How had Jane wound up with him instead?

"He's a corporate lawyer at one of the top law firms in the city," Jane said. "Actually, he's a partner."

Must be loaded.

"He's chatting with Dwight Donahue. Dwight's an aerospace engineer for NASA. Dwight and Quinton made a large enough donation so we could have the reunion here."

So they were both loaded. Miranda remembered a nerdy kid with glasses and his science projects about rockets and solar systems. Most Likely to Become an Astronaut.

She was getting good at this.

She made notes on her post-its. "I think I'm going to win this game."

"Good luck," Jane said.

But not if she stayed with this group. Besides, she was getting uncomfortable.

"C'mon, honey," she said to Parker, taking his hand. "Let's go mingle."

CHAPTER FIVE

It must have been her PI work that made Miranda feel at home asking near strangers personal questions.

She must have talked to over a dozen people.

First was Freddie Quill, who had been the class clown. Miranda learned he had become an English teacher and frequented open mic nights at a downtown comedy club. He was, obviously, Most Likely to Become a Comedian.

A couple of former jocks who used to make snide remarks about her when she went to her locker were next. One was Buster Crabtree. a big linebacker who had put on a lot of weight. He had moved to Cicero, had a wife and five kids, and was driving a sanitation truck.

She'd found Buster in a corner drinking whiskey sours with Barney Hudson, the tight end on the team. After listening to the pair reminisce about their former glory days, Miranda discovered Barney had gone to college and was working for a struggling software company in Glen Ellyn.

They tied for Most Likely to Win the Super Bowl. Hadn't exactly scored that touchdown, had they?

Then there was Victoria Winslow, the girl who played the piccolo in the orchestra. She'd become a kindergarten teacher and had been Most Likely to Join the Philharmonic.

Miranda recalled she'd had a big crush on Quinton Prescott, but who hadn't?

While Miranda chatted with her old schoolmates, the hotel staff shuffled through the crowd serving beverages and the appetizers Parker had predicted. The drinks were exotic. Everything from Old Fashioneds with cane sugar and barrel aged bitters, to martinis with orange saffron, to something with mango, banana, and rum, which was Miranda's choice.

The finger food was exquisite. King crab bites and avocado on a vegetable cucumber roll, chicken wings with a spicy Korean chili sauce, which Miranda loved, even if they were a little messy, and Wagyu beef sliders.

Parker had been right on that score, too. She got only a few bites. She was too busy talking.

Licking her fingers, Miranda chatted with three women she'd recognized as former cheerleaders. They'd also been in Stella La Stella's court when she'd been prom queen. The mean girls. Miranda had received her share of scorn from them back in the day.

Two of them were Keira and Keely, the Roberts twins. They had been the greeters at the door when she and Parker had arrived. Miranda didn't recognize them until they introduced themselves.

Keira had put on a lot of weight and was trying to lose it. Keely had recently had gallbladder surgery. The third was Adelle Bamberger, who was now working in a sub shop and called herself a Sandwich Artist.

Life sure could turn the tables on you, couldn't it?

They'd all had crushes on Quinton Prescott, but wouldn't dare let Stella know about it.

Still, Miranda wished them well and put them down as Most Likely to Become a Model, Most Likely to Become a Movie Star, and Most Likely to Marry a Millionaire.

By the time she deposited her entries in the fish bowl near the podium at the front of the room, she knew she had nailed it. Then the lights turned down low and a DJ began to play music.

"Shall we?" Parker said at her side.

"Nothing I'd like better." Feeling triumphant, she melted into his arms.

He swept her into the crowd on the floor, and under the glittering disco ball, they danced for hours to the strains of Aerosmith, Shania Twain, and Journey.

She smiled up into her handsome husband's face. "Sorry I've been ignoring you most of the evening."

His gaze turned tender. "I've enjoyed watching you. I'm glad you're having a good time."

Glad she wasn't bored. "Who knew interrogation methods could come in handy at a party? At least one without a murder to investigate."

"True." Parker could get a lot of information out of people in a social setting.

But they didn't need to do that any more. This was just for fun.

"Right now, I think I'd like a little privacy." He swept her through the nearest set of glass doors and onto the rooftop terrace.

The terrace was a rectangular shaped space, dotted with lots of little marble top tables for drinks, and plush, white cotton canvas loveseats for intimate after dinner conversations. For safety, a clear Plexiglas banister ran around the perimeter of the area. It was about waist high and had a brushed silver guardrail for extra support that added to the glow.

It was chilly and dark out here, but Miranda could see the lights of the Water Tower, the John Hancock building, and the busy Michigan Avenue below. The city she grew up in had its beautiful side.

There were also a few couples making out in the dark corners.

At the other end of the terrace, she noticed Quinton Prescott and Dwight Donahue talking near the banister and vaguely wondered why they had so much to say to each other after all these years.

Parker drew her close and kissed her hair.

Still moving to the music, she pressed her head against his shoulder. "I never realized how much I love dancing with you."

"Do you?"

"Yeah. It's fun."

Parker's smile turned sly. "If that's the case, we could go across the country and dance our way through the best clubs in every city."

She laughed. "Our new hobby?"

"If you like."

"Or we could go to Hollywood and I could become a professional game show contestant."

He chuckled. "I'm sure you would win every one." Then he bent his head to kiss her.

Drinking in the smell of him, she melted into the kiss and her heart soared as the tall buildings began to whirl around her. Here she was with the love of her life. They were both alive, and they meant to stay that way.

From now on, it would be nothing but joy and happiness, no matter what they decided to do.

Suddenly the music stopped and Jane Anderson's voice came over a loudspeaker.

"Attention everyone. We're about to announce the winner of the Most Likely To contest."

Miranda broke the kiss and let out a little squeal. "Let's see if I won."

Parker's gray eyes gleamed in the low lights. "Wouldn't miss it for the world."

She took Parker's hand and led him back into the main room.

CHAPTER SIX

"Gather in, everyone."

Jane Anderson stood at the podium with the former prom court members at her side. The post-it notes were organized into neat little piles on the table before her. She'd been busy.

"First, I want to say thank you to everyone for coming tonight. We've had a lot of fun, haven't we?"

Everyone applauded and somebody in the back let out a whistle. He'd had a good time.

Jane beamed at the response. "Next I want to thank my committee. I couldn't have done it without them."

She went on for several minutes describing what each person had done. First Keira, then she talked about Keely's contributions. Then Adelle's." When she ran out of things to say, she frowned and peered out into the audience. "Stella? Why aren't you up here?"

Stella emerged from the back of the crowd and made her way up to the podium. "Sorry," she said in a tone that seemed too contrite for her.

Miranda noticed her nose was a little red. She must have been enjoying the fancy libations.

Jane took Stella's hand. "This reunion wouldn't have happened without the help of my co-coordinator." She began heaping praise on Stella.

Miranda couldn't figure out how those two could be so friendly.

She hopped anxiously from foot to foot. Get on with it, Jane. She wanted to know the results of the contest.

Finally, Jane started announcing the winners. The runner up, the third place winner, the second place winner. Each one came up to get a prize and made an embarrassing little speech.

Miranda wanted to roll her eyes. This could take all night.

Finally Jane smiled her biggest smile. "And now first place. The prize is dinner for two at one of the top Michelin rated restaurants in the city."

The crowd oohed.

Miranda elbowed Parker. "Now I can take you out and wine and dine you."

He grinned. "Here it comes."

Jane's eyes glowed. "And the first place winner is—Miranda Steele. Come on up here, Miranda."

"I won. I really won." Miranda couldn't believe it.

As the room broke out in applause, she gave Parker's hand a squeeze and made her way to the podium, wondering what she was going to say for a speech.

Her old friend greeted her with a hug. "Congratulations."

"Thanks, Jane. Thanks so much."

"You deserve it. What a memory you have." Jane gestured toward the terrace. "And here's Quinton to present your prize."

He must have paid for the restaurant passes.

Everyone turned to the glass doors that led outside.

No one appeared.

The applause dwindled into silence.

"Quinton?" Jane said into the mic. "We've just announced the winner."

No response.

Blinking with embarrassment, Jane tried again. "Quinton?"

Nothing.

Jane turned and whispered something to Stella.

With a concerned frown, Stella hurried over to the terrace doors.

"Quinton?" she called. "It's time to present the first place prize."

Then she stepped through the opening and disappeared.

Everyone began to murmur. To Miranda, it felt a little like a Carrie moment—until she heard a loud, blood curdling scream.

A few people started for the doors. Just before they reached them, Stella reappeared, her face pale and bewildered.

For a moment, she couldn't catch her breath.

Then she began to shriek. "Help. Somebody help. There's been an accident."

Now everyone rushed through the doors and onto the terrace.

Miranda picked up her skirts and hurried in the same direction. She saw Parker slip through the opening just ahead of her.

Outside on the terrace, the atmosphere had lost the romantic mood it had had a little while ago. Now the crisp air crackled with panic.

Miranda ran to the Plexiglas banister and leaned over it.

She froze, unable to believe the image she was staring at. Her stomach lurched, and she felt dazed. It was hard to breathe. Was this real?

The body of a man hung over the banister's side, suspended by his necktie. He should have been kicking and struggling, but he wasn't moving at all. He just hung there against the building like a sack of potatoes.

In the darkness, she wouldn't have been able to identify him—if it hadn't been for that cobalt blue tux.

It was Quinton Prescott.

"Grab him," Parker shouted. "Get him back over the rail. Get that tie off of him."

Parker, the linebacker, and the tight end stretched over the Plexiglas and struggled to pull up the body. Finally they managed to get Prescott over. They loosened his tie, pulled it off, and got him to safety.

Such as it was.

They laid him on the terrazzo floor, and the tie slipped away as others gathered around to help.

"I'm a doctor," said one man. "Let me see him."

"I know CPR," shouted another.

But as Miranda neared the body, she could see none of that would do any good.

The face was blue. The swollen tongue hung out of the mouth like a dead fish. There were blood marks in the open staring eyes.

He was gone.

"Someone call 911."

Parker leaned over the body to check for breath and a pulse. But he knew what Miranda did. "We're going to need the police," he said grimly.

They couldn't bring him back.

Slowly Miranda became aware of a sobbing sound.

From behind one of the sofas, Stella La Stella stared down at Prescott, her shoulders bobbing. "What happened? How could this happen?"

Miranda turned the other way and saw Jane standing near one of the marble tables.

Her face was white and filled with sheer disbelief. She opened her mouth as if to ask the same questions Stella had.

And then she collapsed to the floor.

CHAPTER SEVEN

Miranda tried to keep everyone calm, while Parker informed them no one could leave. He didn't say why, but they could probably guess.

Someone found some smelling salts, revived Jane and got her to her feet. Miranda ushered her back into the main hall, sat her down at a table, and got her a drink from the bar.

Jane shook her head at the glass of gin.

She sat staring straight ahead, her back rigid as stone, saying nothing.

She was in shock.

Miranda knew how she felt. She knew what it was like to see your husband die before your eyes. But she'd been lucky. She'd gotten her husband back.

Jane wouldn't.

In that moment, Miranda vowed she would do all she could for her.

Several of the guests wandered into the area and sat down at the tables.

Miranda scanned the doors to make sure no one was trying to get out. Especially Stella. She wished she could talk to Parker, but he was busy on the terrace trying to preserve the crime scene evidence.

Had there been a crime? Or was this an accident, as Stella had said? If so, it was a freak one. Suicide? Quinton Prescott didn't seem like the type to kill himself. He had it all.

But if it wasn't an accident or suicide...then it was murder.

"When are we going to get to go home?" Someone called from a nearby table.

Miranda forced herself not to growl at him. "We have to see what the police say. They'll be here any minute."

"That's what you said an hour ago."

It hadn't been that long, but Miranda wasn't going to argue with the guy.

She didn't need to.

At that moment the far doors opened and a party of uniformed officers and plain clothes people entered the room led by one of the hotel staff. In front of the group was a short woman of about forty in a dark cloth coat.

Miranda did a double take.

The short brown curls had been relaxed and she'd grown them out a bit, giving her a softer look. She had the same square face and boxy body type, but she'd lost weight, and it was evident she'd been working out.

Detective Shirley Templeton.

The woman Miranda had worked with on the Sutherland case. The case that had routed out Adam Tannenburg, the serial killer who had haunted her dreams for months afterwards.

Tannenburg was Mackenzie's father.

Templeton was blinking at her as well. She came up to her like a cautious hound sniffing a stranger. "Miranda Steele? Is that you?"

"Sure is, Templeton." Good to see you." Meaning it, Miranda extended a hand.

Still looking stunned, Templeton shook with her. "What are you doing here?"

Miranda gestured at the half empty room. "It's my high school reunion. Or it was."

Templeton's straight brows rose. "Not sure what to say to that."

"Me, either. So you've been assigned to this case?"

She nodded. "Demarco asked me to take the lead on this one."

Miranda recalled this woman had lost her husband in a fire a couple years ago, and had been working her tail off ever since to become a detective and provide for her little boy. She was happy she was in charge.

Templeton gestured to a skinny guy in a police jacket at her side. "This is John Enzo, my CSI."

So his clothing said. Miranda shook hands with him. "Good to know you."

"Likewise," he said, shifting a large black bag on his shoulder.

Templeton looked around the room. "How many people are here?"

Miranda had guessed at a head count while she'd been waiting. Her former guess was good. "About seventy-five. As far as I know, nobody has left."

Templeton's gaze went to Jane, who was still staring into space.

Miranda lowered her voice. "That's the wife."

Templeton nodded. "Where did the incident take place?"

"Out there on the terrace."

Templeton turned to one of the uniforms. "Keep an eye on her." She pointed to Jane. "And make sure no one leaves."

"Yes, ma'am."

Time to get to work.

Miranda led the detective across the floor and onto the terrace.

CHAPTER EIGHT

Parker rose from the loveseat he'd been sitting on as they approached.

Those who had decided to wait out here looked up at the detective, hoping for answers.

"Detective Templeton." With a protective glance toward Miranda, Parker extended a hand. "I'm sorry to meet again under these circumstances."

"Just what I was about to say." Templeton shook hands, then drew in a weary breath as she looked down at the body. "What happened here?"

Miranda attempted to explain the bizarre event. "Everyone was back in the main room where the coordinator was handing out prizes for a party game."

"Coordinator?"

"Jane Anderson. Actually, she's Jane Prescott. She's the woman at the table out there. The wife."

"I see."

"So Jane called for her husband to give out the last prize, and there was no response. Someone came out here to get him and found him hanging over the banister by his tie."

Templeton peered over the Plexiglas. "You mean over there?"

"That's right, Detective," Parker said, gesturing to the former football players, who were slumped in nearby chairs. "These two gentlemen helped me pull him back over. Unfortunately, we were too late."

Buster Crabtree shook his head. "I don't see Quinton doing himself in. He's just not like that."

"He had everything to live for," Barney Hudson agreed.

"We'll take statements later." Templeton turned to Enzo. "Let's get some photos."

"Yes, ma'am."

While the young man took out his camera and began snapping pictures, Templeton pulled on a pair of blue gloves from her pocket and bent down to study the body.

She checked for a pulse, examined the eyes and the skin, and opened the collar of his shirt.

The ligature marks were an ugly blue.

"Get some shots here," she said to the technician as she rose and her gaze went to Prescott's white silk tie, which was on the floor, the wide end of it still stuck to the banister.

Miranda hadn't had a chance to get a good look at it before. Now she couldn't help going over to the spot and peering down at it.

The silky fabric had been wrapped around the narrow part of one of the banister's classy brushed aluminum handles.

There was a knot holding it in place. Someone had tied it there.

"Hmm," Templeton said, and gestured to her assistant to snap more photos. "We'll need prints of the area as well. "

"Yes, ma'am."

"We're going to have to get this guy to the morgue," Templeton muttered half to herself, and she stepped over to a clear spot near the wall to make a phone call.

Miranda looked over the banister and saw an ambulance parked on the street down below, its lights flashing.

She glanced over at Parker.

His expression told her he had been sitting here all this time thinking about the implications of that knot.

Suicide?

Maybe. But it ruled out accident. That knot didn't tie itself.

"What do you think, Detective?" Buster demanded as soon as Templeton got off the phone.

If the question rattled her, she didn't show it. Miranda thought she was keeping it together pretty well.

"It's too early to say," she said without emotion. "All we know for certain is that Mr. Prescott is deceased."

Buster stared at her as if that was news to him.

"Can we go home now?" Someone whined from one of the couches in the back.

"Not yet. We're going to have to get a statement from everyone in attendance."

A groan went up from the group.

"I have a babysitter waiting for me."

"My teen is home by herself."

"I apologize for the inconvenience. We'll go as quickly as we can."

As Parker came to her side, Miranda expected Templeton to tell them they were no more than witnesses and to stay out of police business.

Instead she lowered her voice and leaned in. "It's going to take all night to interview all these people. How would you two like to help?"

Miranda blinked and turned to Parker. They were supposed to be retired. They were supposed to be ordinary citizens.

"What do you think?"

"It's up to you." His face had a weary look. Here they were, dealing with death again.

But it was just some interrogating. It wasn't as if they'd gotten rusty.

And then she thought of poor Jane Anderson sitting alone at her table staring off into space.

She turned back to Templeton. "Of course, we'll help."

"Grab a notebook and pen from Enzo and we'll get started."

CHAPTER NINE

At Templeton's command, the hotel staff began rearranging the main room into several small partitions.

When the EMTs arrived with a gurney to take Prescott away, Miranda ushered Jane into one of the spaces and told her an officer would speak with her in a bit.

"Where are they taking him?" Jane's big eyes glistened with tears as she watched the EMTs rattle across the floor and out to the terrace.

Had to be honest. "To the morgue."

She looked down at the tablecloth. "So he's gone."

"Yes. I'm sorry." Miranda sat down next to her and dared to touch her hand. "Jane, has Quinton been suffering from depression lately?"

"What do you mean?"

"Was he troubled over anything? Was he down a lot of the time?"

She blinked as if she were trying to translate a foreign language. "Do the police think he killed himself?"

"They haven't drawn any conclusions yet."

Slowly she nodded. "Quinton works a lot. There's a lot of pressure on him."

"Pressure?"

"He's a full partner. He has to keep bringing new clients into the business. It takes long hours."

She was speaking of her husband in present tense. Reality hadn't sunk in yet.

"So he was away from home a good deal."

Jane rubbed her arms. "I know what you're saying, Miranda. Yes, Quinton's job has put a strain on our relationship. But we're working on that. That's why we're planning to get away to Europe next year."

And why Jane couldn't organize the twentieth-year reunion.

"I hate to ask you this, but did Quinton take any substances to help him deal with the job stress?"

Ten minutes seemed to pass before Jane turned to her, large eyes flashing. "I can't believe you said that." Suddenly her eyes filled with tears. "I can't do this anymore."

Guilt flooded Miranda. She knew the kind of pain this poor woman was going through. That was all the interviewing Jane could endure right now.

She got to her feet. "Of course. I'll find someone to take you home."

CHAPTER TEN

After Jane left with an officer, Miranda questioned the Roberts twins, Adele Bamberger, and about twenty others.

She'd wanted a turn at Stella, but Templeton had one of the uniforms talk to her.

It had to be after one when she saw Parker emerge from one of the enclosures looking spent and frustrated.

"I take it you didn't get anything more than I did," she said to him.

He closed his notebook with a grimace. "Most of these people barely remember Quinton Prescott from high school. Others haven't been in contact with him for years. No one knows anything about the man's state of mind of late or any reason why he might take his life."

"Or why someone might take it for him."

Darkly, Parker nodded.

"I thought one of the girls who used to have a crush on Prescott might have a motive, but they said they forgot all about him after graduation. They've had their own troubles to deal with."

"What about the others?"

She shrugged. "No one saw Prescott go onto the terrace tonight. No one knew if he was depressed or using illegal substances. Or had any enemies."

He held up his notebook. "I've made note of a few the police may want to requestion."

"Me, too."

Parker scanned the hall. "There's little more we can do tonight. We'll turn our notes into Detective Templeton and head back to the hotel."

"All right." They'd done all they could.

They found Templeton near the podium talking with her crew. "We're done for tonight. We'll pick things up again in the morning." She turned to Parker and Miranda. "Either of you learn anything?"

"Not really."

Parker handed Templeton their notebooks and pens. "There are a few we marked we feel need more looking into, but there's nothing conclusive."

With a grim nod, Templeton took the notebooks. "We're starting up again at nine tomorrow. If you're staying in town, we'd love your help."

Miranda turned to Parker.

His brow rose as he fixed her with his gaze.

Right. That wasn't why they'd come here.

She turned back to Templeton. "Actually, we've retired from detective work."

Templeton looked as if Miranda had socked her. "You don't say."

"We had some rough cases and decided to call it quits."

That sounded lame, but she couldn't divulge the details of what Santana had tried to do.

Templeton rocked back on her heels and blew out a breath. "Well then, thank you for your help." She took one of the notebooks and scribbled something on a page. She tore it off and handed it to Miranda. "If you change your mind, here's my number."

CHAPTER ELEVEN

It was almost two in the morning when she and Parker got back to their luxury suite in the neighboring hotel.

Feeling exhausted, Miranda tucked the piece of paper with Templeton's cell number under her phone on the nightstand and tugged at her dress.

"I don't know, Parker. Something isn't right about this case."

"Are you referring to the fact that a man was found hanging by his tie over the banister of an elite hotel?" Parker removed his own tie and put it back in its case.

He looked down at it for a moment, as if he were glad it was a bowtie.

"It's more than that." She pulled at her waistband, but it didn't cooperate.

"Such as?" Parker stepped over to her and unzipped the back of her dress, then helped her pull it over her head. He kissed her shoulder.

Ignoring the tingling sensation of his lips, Miranda took the dress and headed for the closet. "Why does a top flight lawyer kill himself while his wife is presenting prizes at their high school reunion?" She put the dress on a hanger and set onto the metal bar with a click.

"Perhaps he didn't like being disqualified." Parker took off his jacket and hung it in the closet beside her dress.

The hotel service would return the tux to the rental place for them tomorrow.

Marching to the dresser, she gave him a mock scowl, then tugged a T-shirt over her head. "You know what I mean. Nobody had any indication that Prescott was depressed or upset, or using drugs for any reason. It just doesn't add up."

"The police have their work cut out for them." He finished undressing and got into bed.

She came around to her side, climbed in beside him, and turned off the light.

Staring up at the ceiling in the darkness, she let out a sigh as she replayed the moments after she'd gone to the podium tonight. The screaming. The stampeding crowd rushing outside to help. Parker and the football players dragging the body back over the banister. Attempting to revive him to no avail.

"Did I tell you Stella La Stella was Quinton Prescott's steady girl in high school?"

"No, you didn't."

"They were a hot number when I was there, and even through graduation, according to Kiera and Keely. Everyone thought they'd get married. But he wound up with Jane instead."

"Did you mention that to Detective Templeton?"

"No. I never really liked Stella. I thought I was biased."

Parker rolled over to stroke her cheek. "I'm glad my lessons are still paying dividends."

Grunting, she gave him a smack on the cheek and snuggled in next to him. "I guess it doesn't matter now."

"The police will figure things out."

"I guess so."

They both grew quiet.

Miranda lay there in the dark, listening to Parker's steady breathing. He sure had more faith in the police than he used to.

No, he just didn't want to get involved in this mess. And why should he? They were retired. They were supposed to be enjoying themselves, not getting involved in a suicide case that might be a murder.

She had to remember that.

She closed her eyes and tried to forget about tonight. A good night's sleep was what she needed.

Maybe they'd do some sightseeing tomorrow before they left town. Maybe they'd go off to some new place. Take a cruise up Lake Michigan, maybe. Visit the Wisconsin Dells. That made her think of the waterfalls in the North Georgia Mountains.

She began to drift. Deeper. Deeper. Suddenly, she felt as if she were floating down a beautiful winding river through craggy rock formations and cool, deep green forests.

She was seeking peace. Resolution. Comfort.

As her boat moved over the water, she gazed at the shoreline, a strip of beach and tall trees growing alongside it. A moment ago it had been sunny. Now the sky was turning dark and the tree trunks grew thick and tangled.

Along the shore wild beasts appeared. Grizzly bears and tigers. A shaggy lion growled at her from the dense undergrowth. Where was she?

And then she saw him standing between the trees in the undergrowth.

Tall and muscular, he was dressed in a loincloth. His shaggy blond hair hung to his shoulders. His vivid green eyes were wild, his face and chest smeared with blood. In his hand he held a spear with a long sharp arrowhead.

As she floated past, he pointed it at her. "I will make you suffer for what you did to me."

With a cry, she started awake and glared at the clock, her heart pounding.

Four in the morning.

She turned her head. Parker was sound asleep. At least she hadn't kicked him.

"Damn you, Tannenburg," she whispered to the darkness. "Get out of my head."

Angry with her own subconscious, she lay back down. She hadn't had a bad dream for weeks. Was what happened to Quinton Prescott bringing her old demons back? Maybe it was time for another session with Dr. Wingate.

But as she closed her eyes again, now all she could see was the image of Jane Anderson Prescott sitting alone at that table in the Royal Rose Hotel reception room, lost and bewildered and in pain.

Suddenly she couldn't stand the idea of walking away from her husband's possible murder.

She had to do something.

She reached for her phone and tapped in the number on the paper she'd put under it. Then she sent a text.

We'll be there in the morning.

CHAPTER TWELVE

Miranda awoke the next morning to the smell of coffee, delicious and black. Not quite as good as Parker's special imported blend, but good enough to make her mouth water.

She opened her eyes and found Parker standing beside the bed holding two steaming cups. He was bathed and dressed casually in a gray polo shirt and charcoal slacks. The light from the window behind him gave him an otherworldly glow.

Smiling she sat up and took the cup from him. "Are you my guardian angel?"

He kissed her forehead and sat down beside her. "I like to think so."

She drank in his love, once again overjoyed that he was alive.

Then her cell buzzed and his gaze went to the screen.

It was a message from Templeton. Uh oh.

Parker picked up the phone and read it, as well as the other one.

His jaw went tight. "You sent a text to Detective Templeton at four in the morning?"

She stared at him, not knowing what to say.

"I thought we were past this sort of thing." He put the phone back down.

Yes. They were. She set her cup next to the phone on the nightstand.

His anger rippling through her, she dragged a hand through her hair. What had she been thinking? "I'm sorry, Parker. I had a bad dream last night."

"Another nightmare?" His tone turned to concerned.

"Yeah." She picked up her phone.

The message from Templeton included Jane's address and said she was going there this morning to follow up.

Miranda groaned. "I shouldn't have sent that text last night. I just couldn't stop thinking about Jane. I feel so bad for her and what she must be going through. I'll tell Templeton I made a mistake."

Parker grabbed her hand. "Miranda. Were you going to meet Detective Templeton alone this morning?"

She blinked at him. "No. I don't think so. I don't know. I was half asleep."

His eyes narrowed. "Don't you think I'm feeling the same things for that poor woman as you are?"

She hadn't thought about that, but of course, he must be. Parker had been through the same pain she had. He'd thought she was dead, too.

"Let me call Templeton. I'll explain it to her." Somehow.

"Miranda," he said again, this time in his boss voice. "If you want to work this case so badly, I won't say no."

Huh? "Really?"

"If you think you can handle it."

She had been thinking he was the one who couldn't handle it.

"I simply want you to tell me what you're thinking." He held up her phone. "And don't make decisions without consulting me."

He took her breath.

But she got his point. "Okay. You're right. But yes, I do want to help out on this case."

"Very well." Rising, he handed her back her phone. "Then let's get going."

CHAPTER THIRTEEN

After picking up breakfast sandwiches and coffee to go at one of the hotel's restaurants, which Parker insisted on, they hopped into the Jaguar and headed west.

There were accidents on the expressway, so Parker took a detour across the river and under the L tracks, which ran all the way out to Laramie and through some dicey looking neighborhoods. The traffic was as bad as Atlanta's, but after the curving avenues and hilly roads of the North Georgia Mountains, Miranda wondered how the streets here could be so flat and straight.

Even though she had grown up here.

The address Templeton had texted was in the ritzy part of River Forest, and after about forty-five minutes, Parker turned north, then west again and into a neighborhood of large brick homes whose owners obviously had well paying jobs.

He slowed in front of a sprawling English Tudor with spiky rooftops and gothic windows.

"This is the place?"

"It's the address Templeton gave you."

Then they were here.

Nice house. Miranda spotted the detective's old gray Tahoe in the drive. "She's here."

Parker pulled into the driveway right behind a second vehicle. A gold Impala with a vanity plate reading "LA STELLA."

"Wonder who that belongs to," Miranda smirked.

"And why she's here."

She reached for the handle. "Let's go find out."

As Miranda walked up to the front steps at Parker's side, it felt like old times. Nothing had ever excited her more than working cases with her smart sexy husband—except making love to him. But this case was temporary, she reminded herself.

They were only here to help out.

They reached the elegant arched front door and rang the bell.

After a moment, the door opened and Stella appeared, her thick dark hair falling in loose curls to her shoulders. She had on tight black stretch pants and a robin's egg blue knit top with long sleeves and a twist at the front. It was just casual wear, but she looked like a lingerie model.

Miranda noted her red eyes and nose.

Stella eyed Miranda with confusion laced with a hint of disdain. "What are you two doing here?"

Nice welcome.

"Detective Templeton asked for our help," Miranda told her flatly.

Stella shook her head. "I don't think Jane's in any condition to answer more questions." She was about to close the door on them.

Miranda stuck out an arm to stop her. "You do want to find out what happened to her husband, don't you?"

Oozing his Southern charm, Parker stepped closer to the threshold. "Stella, I'm sure Jane would welcome any information we might be able to uncover."

Stella turned to him and blinked, and Miranda could see she was fighting the natural female reaction to Parker. And thinking about how her lack of cooperation might be interpreted.

After a moment, she stepped back. "All right, if you must. But don't upset her."

"We'll be delicate," Parker promised.

They entered a tall two-story foyer with a parquet floor, gothic stained windows, and a carved walnut stairway that disappeared somewhere high above.

"She's in the den." Stella led them across a hardwood floor, past a huge elegant living room and into a smaller one.

This one had pretty blue walls, a large picture window with a view of a big backyard, and cozy looking furniture.

Dressed in dark sweats and a gray drape-wrap cardigan, Jane was nestled in the corner of a brown leather L-shaped couch. Next to three coffee cups, a box of tissues sat on the rustic coffee table in front of her. From the number of crushed balls around her, it looked like she had worked her way through about half of it.

Wearing the camel-colored suit Miranda remembered her in, Templeton sat beside Jane, a notebook in her lap and a briefcase on the floor.

Jane blew her nose and stared up at Miranda and Parker with her big doe like eyes. "I didn't know you were coming over."

Miranda's heart melted for her. "Detective Templeton asked us to. I hope that's okay."

"Sure. I guess." She gave a sad little laugh. "We were just talking about my blog."

Tossing her thick black hair over her shoulder, Stella picked up the tissues and put them in the trash. "I told you not to worry about the blog today, Jane."

Miranda glanced at Parker. "Blog?"

"I have a mommy blog," Jane explained.

"Mommy blog?"

Jane waved the tissue in her hand and began to chatter. "Oh, I know some people don't like that term, but that's what it is. It's called 'Me and My Boys.' I started it a few years ago as sort of an online journal. I talk about Reid and Quinton Jr's ballgames, their homework, what we're having for dinner, how I organize my day. That sort of thing. I'm up to a few hundred followers. Lately I've been writing about the reunion, and all the preparations, and the Most Likely To game. I promised my readers I would tell them who won today."

"It doesn't matter," Stella insisted as she settled into a nearby armchair. "They'll understand."

Tearing up, Jane reached for another tissue. "I hope so."

She was sublimating. Using the trivial to keep her mind off the tragic. Miranda was well acquainted with the process. And she knew Templeton had gotten her onto a personal topic to gain trust.

"We'd like to go over some details with you, if we may," Parker said smoothly.

Jane blinked up at him as if she'd just noticed he was here. "Oh. I guess so."

Stella popped up from her chair. "Coffee. You need coffee." And she turned and hurried out of the room.

Running away from something?

Miranda gave Parker a look of suspicion. He returned one that said he agreed.

She gave him a nod and followed Stella down the hall to the kitchen.

CHAPTER FOURTEEN

The kitchen was all white cabinets and shiny tiles with a walnut trim running around the edge of the ceiling. The far end held a huge marble table with eight tall iron back chairs.

As if she didn't realize Miranda was there, Stella went to the light granite countertop, retrieved the carafe from the coffee maker, and turned to the sink.

When she saw Miranda in the doorway, she started and pressed a hand to her throat. "Miranda. I didn't realize you'd followed me."

Didn't she? "I thought you could use some help."

"I don't think I do. Why don't you go back to the den." She moved to the sink and pushed up the handle of the curved bronze faucet to fill the pot with filtered water.

Miranda went to the opposite corner and began opening cabinets until she found one with cups. She took out two and set them on the corner. "Actually, I'd like to chat a bit, since we didn't get to do that last night."

Stella didn't bother to suppress a huff of annoyance. "All right. What do you want to know?"

She needed to phrase her words carefully. Stella could be slippery. "For one thing, I was wondering how you and Jane got together again after all these years."

Stella opened her mouth in surprise, then turned toward another cabinet and took out a canister of coffee. As she spooned the grounds into a filter, she said, "I guess it was about a year ago. I was on the train into the city and I sat down right next to Quinton. I didn't recognize him until he asked if it was me."

"Really?"

"Yes, isn't that wild? We joked about it and said it was a fluke of Fate."

She bet it was.

Stella got the coffee machine going and continued. "Well, we talked and you know, caught up. I told him what I'd been up to, and he told me he was working for Sikora and Vogel downtown, and that he had married Jane. I was so shocked. Not that Jane wasn't a catch or anything. She's a sweet person. You know that. You were her best friend until you left school."

Had to bring that up again.

Miranda resisted the urge to inform her she had her GED, had taken some college courses, had had intensive PI training at the Parker Agency, and knew how to lay asphalt.

"He told me Jane was getting a committee together for the reunion party, and invited me to dinner to talk to her about it. I ended up volunteering to help. We spent a lot of hours working together and grew close. She's a good friend. Really, she is."

So she kept saying. "Sounds like you and Jane and Quinton all became friends."

"Yes, we did. We had a lot of fun together. Quinton worked late a lot, but Jane and I had many dinners together right there at that table while we were working on the reunion. Keira and Keely were here a lot, too." She pointed at the big marble slab.

Keira and Keely. The Roberts twins, who'd helped with planning the party.

"I got to know her boys pretty well. Reid is in fifth grade. He's a math whiz. Quinton Junior loves soccer. He's in seventh grade."

Are you sure you didn't read that on the mommy blog? Miranda wondered. "Where are the boys, by the way?"

"Jane's mother came to stay with her last night. She took them to her house after Detective Templeton called."

Poor kids.

Stella went over to the table and picked up one of the silver bundles left over from the party. "Jane and I worked so hard on the reunion. I thought things went really well last night, up until—" She put her hand over her mouth.

Was she choking back real tears?

Pulling herself together, Stella hurried back to the counter. Quickly she retrieved a tray from a lower cabinet and started to put everything on it. "The coffee's done. I'd better get it in there."

Before Miranda could stop her, she was down the hall.

Grunting with annoyance, Miranda followed.

She reached the den in time to see Stella set the cups on the table and pour the fresh coffee into them. Then she refreshed the cups that were already there.

Everyone stared down at the table.

Nobody wanted coffee.

Stella set the pot and tray down and took her place in the armchair next to Jane.

After a moment of silence, Templeton cleared her throat and turned to Jane. "There isn't an easy way to say this, but I've got a search warrant from my boss. He wants me to look over your place. I hope you don't mind."

So that was Templeton's reason for coming here. Miranda was glad she and Parker were here to assist instead of a bunch of uniformed cops.

Jane stared at Templeton as if she were coming out of a dream. "I suppose I don't really have a choice, do I?"

Stella popped up again, a mother bear protecting her cub. "Do we have to do this now?"

"I'm afraid so."

"It's all right, Stella." Jane got to her feet. "Let's just get it over with."

CHAPTER FIFTEEN

They decided to split up.

Templeton asked Stella to show her the downstairs rooms, while Jane took Miranda and Parker up the walnut staircase to the upper floors.

The detective hadn't said what she was looking for, but Miranda knew it was anything that could prove Quinton Prescott had been depressed or upset enough to kill himself last night.

They started with the bedroom at the end of the hall.

The walls were painted with a light gray Latex, and covered with posters of soccer stars in action. In the corner stood a white beadboard bookcase filled with basketballs, soccer balls, and books about sports stars.

Near a window was a bed with wheels and a spread that made it look like a race car.

"This is Quinton Junior's room " Jane said as she stepped into the space. "I slept in here with both of the boys last night. Mother must have made the bed before she left. She took the boys to her house for the day."

"So Stella told me." At least that much checked out. "We'll have to go through it."

They probably wouldn't find anything in here, but they had to follow protocol.

"If that's what the police insist on." Jane sighed and sank down onto the mattress.

Parker touched Miranda's arm. "I'll take the closet."

"Okay." While Parker went to the corner, she pulled open the top drawer of the dresser.

She went through the neatly folded underwear. Nothing unusual here. Next drawer. T-shirts in loud colors with sports logos and cute sayings. Next, the corresponding shorts and sleepwear.

The bottom drawer held notebooks with homework assignments and tests from school. Tucked in the back corner, she found a pair of dirty socks.

Using her thumb and forefinger, she pulled them out. "You might want to do something with these."

Jane rolled her eyes. "Now why didn't he put those in the hamper." She crossed the room, took them from Miranda, and tossed them into a white wicker basket.

Parker came out of the closet with a magazine. "I found this on the floor."

The cover featured gruesome cartoon figures with claws and fangs in what looked like a fight to the death.

Jane let out a huff. "I told Quinton Junior he couldn't have that comic book. It's too violent." She snatched it out of Parker's hand and tucked it under her arm.

Miranda wondered if the incident would wind up in Jane's blog.

Ten-year-old Reid's room featured dark blue walls, a colorful duvet with a geometric pattern, a rope ladder hanging from the ceiling, Legos near a toy chest, and pictures of Einstein on the walls. They found much of the same in here, except this time the boy had hidden chewing gum under a desk and a bag of candy in one of the drawers.

Again, Jane sighed, taking the bag from Miranda. "He has such a sweet tooth, but he's had so many cavities lately."

They went through the kid's bathrooms, which Jane's mother must have cleaned before she left. They were too spotless for young boys. Miranda and Parker searched hall closets, a guest room, and finally reached the master bedroom.

Jane hesitated in the hallway.

Thinking of how hard it had been for her to sleep in their bed when she thought Parker was gone, Miranda put a hand on her arm. "It's okay." She eyed the neighboring door. "Is that the master bath?"

Jane nodded.

"I'll check the bedroom while you two go through the bathroom," Parker offered.

Miranda was grateful for his tenderness. "Sounds good."

The master bath was all walnut and charcoal tile and brushed silver. There were linens and soap. Bath salts and fragrances. Shampoos and conditioners.

While Miranda went through drawers, Jane stood near the glass shower hugging herself, still holding the forbidden magazine and bag of candy.

Good time for some questions. "I was surprised to learn you and Stella were friends," Miranda said, trying to sound as if she were just making conversation.

Jane blinked as if coming out of a trance. "Oh, why?"

"You know. Things were kind of different in high school."

Jane's large eyes widened. Then she shook her head. "That was a long time ago."

Wondering if Jane remembered how mean Stella could be back then, Miranda opened a floor-to-ceiling cabinet and shifted through towels and bath cloths and toilet tissue." Did you keep in touch all these years?"

"No. I think it was about six months or so ago. Anyway, one day she showed up on my doorstep."

"Oh?" That was different from what Stella had told her.

"I had sent out messages on social media for anyone who was interested in helping to plan the reunion to contact me. She decided to volunteer."

Miranda was about to ask how Stella got her address when she opened the medicine cabinet. "Whoa."

Frowning, Jane came to her side and peered over her shoulder. "What is it?"

"A lot of bottles in here." She read some of the labels. "Creatine, B12, beetroot powder."

"Quinton was something of a health nut. It was part of his routine. He used to wake up at five, go downstairs and work out in our home gym. Then he'd come up here to shower and take a handful of pills. He liked to stay fit."

Maybe a little obsessive about it. Miranda moved the bottles aside. "Belladonna?"

"Oh, that was for his hay fever."

Really. Behind the herbal supplements was a big bottle of acetaminophen. Miranda pushed it to the side and found a prescription.

"Oxycodone?" She picked up the bottle.

Jane had to step closer to look at it. "Yes. Quinton broke his toe last year. When he was getting off the treadmill, of all things. The doctor gave him that for pain, but he didn't take much of it."

Apparently not. The prescription was for thirty pills, and it looked like at least two-thirds of them were still in the bottle. The date matched what Jane had just said.

Miranda took note of the doctor's name and put the bottle back in the cabinet. If Quinton Prescott was depressed and wanted to kill himself, an oxycodone overdose would have been easier than throwing himself over a banister.

She thought of what Stella had said. "Was taking the train to work also part of Quinton's routine?"

Jane looked surprised at the question. "Yes. He drove to the Oak Park station every day and took it into the city. He liked to spend the time working instead of sitting in traffic."

"I suppose he came home the same way?"

"Sometimes. He worked long hours and he'd often get a room in the city. Why?"

"I just wondered." She also wondered how Prescott "worked out" on the days he stayed in the city. And whether Stella had been part of his routine.

Then she glanced in the mirror and saw Parker had been standing in the doorway watching her.

"Nothing in the bedroom," he said.

"Nothing here, either." Nothing that was conclusive, anyway.

She closed the medicine cabinet and they went back downstairs where they found Templeton finishing up in the dining room. She had nothing to report, either.

"Thank you for your time, Mrs. Prescott," she said to Jane, and everyone shook hands and left.

Stella looked relieved as she closed the door behind them.

Now alone, the three of them moved to the police issued Tahoe and stood on the driveway in a huddle.

Templeton shook her head. "There wasn't any indication of the husband's depression that I could see."

Miranda shoved her hands into the pockets of her jacket. "There was a big bottle of oxycodone in the medicine cabinet, but Quinton hadn't taken many of them."

Templeton's brows rose. "Really?"

"Jane said the doctor prescribed them when he broke his toe last year. I'd like to check that out."

"Good idea. We're having a meeting at the station in about an hour. You both are welcome to attend."

Miranda turned to Parker. He seemed interested in the idea.

"We'll follow you there," he said to Templeton.

Miranda wanted to let out a breath of relief. There were too many loose ends to drop this case now.

Templeton nodded. "See you in a bit, then."

And they climbed into the Jaguar and pulled out of the driveway.

CHAPTER SIXTEEN

"Sorry you didn't get to ask Jane your questions," Miranda said as they rolled back through the neighborhood.

Parker came to a halt at a stop sign, then turned left. "It seems you handled that instead. Did Stella tell you a different story about how she connected with Jane after high school? Other than showing up on her doorstep?"

Miranda frowned. He couldn't have heard all that from the bathroom doorway. He'd been searching the bedroom when she'd brought up the subject to Jane.

Then she narrowed her eyes at her sneaky husband. "There was a door leading to the master bedroom that was ajar."

"Very observant," Parker said smugly.

She was wondering if he was into this case more than he let on.

Parker often seemed to have psychic powers, but this time it was his deductive skills in action. He'd heard more of her conversation with Jane than she'd thought.

Miranda watched the taillights of Templeton's Tahoe as they paused at another stop sign. "Stella said she met Quinton on the train into the city about a year ago."

"Which was why you asked about his mode of transportation to work."

"Yep. But, as you overheard, Jane said Stella showed up on her doorstep to help with the reunion committee about six months ago."

Parker turned right and followed Templeton down a side street lined with more expensive looking solid brick homes. "It could be Jane misremembered the details. She's understandably upset."

"And probably not thinking straight," Miranda had to admit.

He came to another stop sign. "Or Prescott could have been having an affair with Stella behind Jane's back."

"Yeah."

But now that Parker had spoken her secret suspicion out loud, it sounded flat.

They turned onto Harlem and picked up speed.

Miranda drummed her fingers on her lap. "If that's true, then it was Jane who had a motive to do away with her husband. But she was busy with the reunion all night. It was Stella who found the body. Jane was at the podium."

"And Stella would have more of a motive to kill Jane than Prescott."

"Right." Miranda's shoulders slumped as they passed a ball field.

"On the surface."

She turned to him. "What are you thinking?"

"That it's too early to draw conclusions."

She let out a sigh. Parker's famous patience.

Reading her frustration, he reached over and patted her hand. "Let's see what the evidence the police gathered last night tells us about that theory."

CHAPTER SEVENTEEN

They reached the tall beige brick building that was the Larrabee police station in forty minutes and followed the Tahoe into the parking lot.

After finding spaces among the squad cars, they got out and went in the back way.

The homicide unit looked just as Miranda remembered it. A patchwork of bland gray partitions forming cubes filled with utilitarian metal desks, squeaky chairs, and posters of the killers the officers were hunting.

It even had the same stale coffee smell.

"How the heck are you two?"

At the sound of the familiar voice, Miranda turned and recognized the skinny frame and thinning curls of Sergeant Thomas Demarco, who ran the division.

Because it was Sunday, he was clad in a green knit shirt and khaki slacks instead of his usual shirt and tie. But his hair seemed sparser, and there were more lines in his face.

Police work was stressful.

"Good to see you, Sergeant." Parker extended a hand.

"And you." Demarco took his signature toothpick out of his mouth and shook with Parker. Then he did the same with Miranda. "It's good to see you both."

He was grinning, but his sharp cop eyes took her in, as if he was wondering how she and Parker were still together.

Their relationship almost hadn't survived the stunt Parker had pulled with Demarco the last time they'd been here. But that was water under the bridge, and right now it seemed like light years ago.

Demarco nodded toward his new detective. "Templeton here tells me you've retired?"

"A short time ago," Parker said, as if it didn't really matter.

"Sorry to drag you into this case, but we're glad to have the help."

"We'll do what we can," Miranda assured him.

"Come on over to the conference room. We just ordered lunch."

Miranda glanced up at the clock on the wall. It was already after one. No wonder lunch sounded good.

With the industrial carpet muting their steps, the three of them followed Demarco around a few corners and into a large rectangular room with a long conference table that took up most of the space. The table was surrounded by mesh ergonomic office chairs, and a projector screen hung from the wall.

At the far end of the table, Detective Robert Kadera had his hand in a big brown paper sack. As soon as he saw he had company, he pulled it out and grinned at them with his straight white teeth.

"Well, well, well, if it isn't my old pals, Steele and Parker."

Last time they'd been here, Kadera had called them celebrities. He'd grown friendlier since their first encounter with him, but they had never been old pals.

He was sucking up.

He wiped his hand on a napkin and came around the table to shake. "Good to see you both. And to have you on this case."

"We're glad to help," Parker said, sounding like he meant it.

Kadera was also in casual garb, a white polo shirt and a pair of gray dockers. But he still wore his dark hair in the Elvis style pompadour he favored. Some things never changed.

Demarco gestured toward the bag. "You have some extra sandwiches for our guests?"

"Sure do. I thought you'd be coming. Hope you like deli fare."

"We're not picky." Miranda took the wrapped sandwich Kadera handed her and pulled out a chair.

It turned out to be a Turkey Club with fresh lettuce and tomato, and spicy mustard. Parker got the tuna salad on rye, and Templeton wound up with a Reuben. There were chips and sodas handed around as well.

Once everyone was settled and munching, Demarco turned to Templeton. "How'd it go this morning, Detective?"

Looking pleased with having been assigned the lead, Templeton swallowed her bite of sandwich, wiped her mouth, and consulted her notebook. "Mrs. Prescott stated her husband was under a great deal of work stress, but as far as she knew, nothing else was bothering him. I searched the entire Prescott house with Steele and Parker's help, but we didn't find much. I did discover Mrs. Prescott has a mommy blog."

Kadera's lip curled. "Mommy blog?"

"It's a blog she writes about her experiences raising her two sons. There might be something in it. She was worried about not posting today. Her friend was telling her it wasn't necessary."

"Which friend was that?"

"Stella La Stella."

Demarco gave Templeton a questioning look.

"She was Mrs. Prescott's co-coordinator on the reunion committee. Seems they got close while working on it."

Demarco crunched on a potato chip and nodded.

From his body language, Miranda got the impression this case was some sort of test for Templeton. As if Demarco was making sure she could handle being in charge of a possible murder investigation. She obviously wanted to prove herself to her boss.

Miranda could relate to how Templeton must feel.

"As I said," Templeton continued, "there was nothing to indicate depression or suicidal tendencies on the victim's part. In fact, just the opposite. He was pretty heavy into physical fitness."

Demarco slurped his root beer. "Interesting. Good work."

"Thank you, sir. Steele did find something of note, though."

"Oh?"

Templeton nodded. "Oxycodone in the medicine cabinet of the master bedroom. And a bottle of belladonna."

Both Demarco and Kadera turned to Miranda with raised brows.

She put down her Turkey Club. "It might not mean anything. Mrs. Prescott told me the belladonna was for allergies. The oxycodone was prescribed by a doctor after Prescott broke his little toe a few months ago. From the look of the bottle, he didn't take much of the prescription. Mrs. Prescott confirmed that."

"But those substances were on hand," Kadera said.

"They were handy if someone wanted to use them." Miranda looked at Templeton, then at Kadera, then at Demarco.

She cleared her throat.

Demarco's frown turned wary. "What is it, Steele?"

"There was a discrepancy between something Ms. La Stella and Mrs. Prescott told me."

"What kind of discrepancy?"

"I asked each of them how they got together again after high school. Stella said about a year ago, she met Prescott on the train to work, and he invited her to dinner. Jane told me it was six months ago, and that Stella showed up on her doorstep one day. She assumed it was in response to her asking for help with the reunion on social media."

Looking skeptical, Demarco balled up his empty sandwich wrapper and stuffed it into the paper bag. "That could be a faulty memory on either of the women's part."

"It could be."

"Kind of bold just to show up uninvited," Kadera said. "How'd she get the address?"

"Jane might have given that out in her post." Though that wasn't smart. Or confirmed.

Miranda glanced at Parker.

He returned a steady look, as if to say he'd read her mind and agreed with her.

It was time to spill the beans.

"Is there something else, Steele?" Demarco wanted to know.

Templeton was looking at her in wonder, as well.

Miranda drew in a breath. "Stella La Stella was Quinton Prescott's steady girlfriend in high school."

Demarco sat back in his chair with a squeak while Kadera let out a low whistle.

But Templeton looked hurt. "Why didn't you tell me that, Steele?"

Miranda grimaced. "I didn't like Stella very much in high school. She was the most popular girl in our class. She was homecoming queen, prom queen. You know the type."

Templeton nodded as if she'd had her own Stella La Stella once upon a time. "Was Prescott the prom king?"

"Yep."

The room fell silent.

Miranda turned to Templeton in half an apology. "I thought my feelings would taint the investigation. But after that confession from the two women this morning, I'm not so sure."

The men looked at her. They knew there was more. So did Templeton.

"What do you mean?" Demarco prompted.

"Jane told me Prescott worked long hours for his job. He's a partner in a top law firm downtown. She confirmed he'd take the train into the city to get extra work done during the commute, and that he sometimes got a room and stayed overnight. I got the impression that was more often than not."

Demarco took a toothpick holder out of his front pocket and put one in his mouth. "And you think he might have been spending his nights doing...a different type of work?"

"Could be."

"You think he might have been cheating on his wife?" Templeton said. Now she seemed more intrigued by that possibility than disappointed Miranda hadn't told her the details.

"It's possible."

Demarco pointed his toothpick at her. "And you think he might have been cheating with La Stella."

Miranda spread her hands. "They had a lot of chemistry in high school. And I'm not talking about the class. As I recall, Stella wasn't the type to be picky about who she slept with back then."

"Did Prescott know that?" Kadera asked.

"I'm not sure. Didn't stop him from going steady with her. I heard her in the hall one time saying he was 'the one'." She'd just remembered that.

And how Prescott and La Stella used to saunter down the halls arms around each other, kissing and making goo-goo eyes.

Used to make her sick.

Kadera chewed thoughtfully on the last bite of his sandwich. "So she meets Prescott on the train one day, starts up an affair with him, then goes and befriends his wife? That's downright brazen."

But not out of character for someone like Stella. Except it didn't quite fit.

"And why would she kill him?" Demarco asked.

"Maybe he wanted to end the relationship," Templeton offered. "Maybe he told her he wasn't getting a divorce for her. That happens often enough."

Nodding, Kadera took a sip of cola and gestured with his forefinger. "So she makes friends with the wife to stay close enough to have an opportunity to off him."

Demarco seemed unconvinced. "It's a scenario, but we have nothing to prove it. Or anything else at this point. Let's go over the evidence we have."

CHAPTER EIGHTEEN

They cleaned up the lunch debris, turned down the conference room lights, and Kadera projected the crime scene photos from last night onto the screen on the wall.

"These are from the banister on the rooftop terrace."

Miranda's Turkey Club didn't settle well as she eyed the Plexiglas barrier and its brushed silver guardrail with Prescott's white tie dangling from it.

Kadera opened a folder and read from it. "Fingerprints have been identified from DMV records. The only prints on the Plexiglas were Prescott's, La Stella's, one of the servers, and Dwight Donahue."

Dwight Donahue.

It took a moment for Miranda to place him. Right, the dude from NASA. A former classmate. She'd seen him talking with Prescott when she and Parker were on the terrace. She still couldn't believe the gawky geek from high school had become so successful.

"Servers from last night confirmed Prescott was drinking heavily," Kadera added.

Parker pointed at the projected photo. "Which explains those fingerprints on the banister."

"Yes."

"And that leaves Stella's and Donahue's to explain," Templeton pointed out.

Parker studied the photo, the wheels in his sharp investigator's mind turning. "It's reasonable to assume that Stella leaned over the banister when she discovered Prescott hanging from it last night."

"Let's see." Kadera flipped back a few photos and enlarged the picture.

There were handprint smears on the Plexiglas where Stella must have braced herself.

"Are those her prints?" Miranda asked.

Kadera consulted his file again. "Sure are. Donahue's are over here." He pointed several feet away with a laser pointer.

Templeton was consulting her phone. "I've got a transcription of the interview with Donahue from last night. He claims he was chatting casually with Prescott on the terrace just before the contest winners were announced."

Demarco frowned. "Contest winners?"

"The Most Likely To... game," Miranda explained. "Everyone was guessing who back in high school had been Most Likely To become president, or a movie star, or a rock star. That sort of thing."

"It was both an ice breaker and a contest," Parker added.

"Whoever guessed the most correctly won."

"And who was the winner?" Kadera said.

"Me."

Kadera let out a laugh. "That's what you get for inviting PIs to your party. What did you win?"

Miranda shrugged. "I never got the prize. Prescott was supposed to present it, but of course, he didn't appear. That was when Stella went out to the terrace and found him."

"That's what the other witnesses state, as well," Templeton said.

Kadera studied the photo on the screen. "Maybe he was drunk enough to fall over the side of the building."

Demarco scoffed. "But sober enough to tie that knot in his tie? I don't buy that."

"Yeah. Me, either."

Miranda thought a moment. "Did you get any prints off the tie?"

Kadera shook his head. "Not yet. The silk is proving to be tricky, but the lab is working on it."

The room fell silent.

As everyone stared up at the photo, trying to see some revelation in it, Miranda felt the familiar sensation of futility she'd had on so many cases. Why had she volunteered her and Parker for this one? All she'd done was offer speculation that hadn't done much good.

No, she knew why. It was for Jane. She wanted to help her friend, but she couldn't even do that.

There was a knock, and everyone turned as the CSI tech from last night appeared at the door.

"Yes, Enzo?" Demarco said.

"Sorry to interrupt, sir. But the preliminary autopsy is in from the ME."

"Thank you. Give us a summary."

Enzo swallowed nervously and consulted the printout in his hand. "COD was asphyxiation via constriction of the airway, compounded by constriction of the carotid artery, interrupting blood flow to the brain. The deceased would have been unconscious within fifteen seconds and dead in five to ten minutes."

Five to ten minutes. Miranda thought of Stella rushing out to the terrace, then rushing back in. That wasn't enough time for Stella to have done it. Not to mention the how. There were still people on the terrace just before Jane gave out the prizes, so she couldn't have done it then.

"What we expected," Demarco said. "Anything else?"

"Blood alcohol level was through the roof."

"Confirms the testimony of the servers. Is there anything there about a broken little toe?"

"Little toe?" Frowning, Enzo shuffled through the report. "Nothing about a toe. Oh, but a large amount of oxycodone was found in the deceased's blood stream."

Miranda's throat went tight. "Oxycodone?"

"That would make it even harder to tie that knot himself," Parker said darkly.

Demarco agreed. "Yep. I'd say this is looking more and more like murder."

Everyone was quiet for a long moment. Then Demarco closed his laptop and got to his feet. "All right, people. Let's get to digging. Kadera, check out the toe."

"Yes, sir."

"Templeton, you and the PIs work on the oxycodone prescription, the mommy blog, and whatever else you can think of."

Templeton pushed back her chair. "On it, sir."

"We need to get this thing wrapped up. We've got pressure from the higher ups and the media to give the public some answers."

CHAPTER NINETEEN

While Kadera ran off to the Medical Examiner's and Demarco disappeared into his office, Templeton found Miranda and Parker a big double cube with a wraparound desk and two chairs.

She had an IT guy set up a couple of standard issue laptops for them, and they went to work.

Parker followed up on the oxycodone prescription while Miranda opened a browser and searched for *Me and My Boys*, Jane's mommy blog.

It came up right away.

There were a lot of articles. Jane had been posting about three to six times a week for five years.

Miranda started plowing through them.

There were recipes for everything from chicken soup to slime. Lots of photos of both boys growing up. Quinton Jr. had his father's blond curls and seemed to smile a lot. Reid had his mother's big brown eyes, but was more serious. There was a picture chronicle of the remake of the boys' bedrooms—the ones Miranda and Parker had searched that morning. There were videos of family outings and trips to local parks and museums. Prescott appeared in a few of those. And then there were practical posts on how to help children with their homework, how to set and enforce bedtimes, and special considerations when bringing up boys.

For a while, Miranda got lost watching videos of Quinton Jr. kicking goals in his soccer games. He was a big boy, and while competing he wore an expression that said he took his role as a forward seriously. In another video, brainy Reid was making slime with his mother in the kitchen Miranda had stood in that morning.

She had to smile as he carefully explained that slime was a non-Newtonian fluid.

Then Miranda got into earlier posts about Jane's "personal journey," as she called it. Here she detailed more intimate things. Her feelings about motherhood. Her joys, her hopes for her boys, her fears.

The one thing she didn't say much about was her marriage.

And then Miranda read something that made her back go straight.

"Parker," she said over her shoulder.

"Hmm?" He'd been deep in thought.

"Take a look at this." She pointed to her screen.

Parker rolled his chair over and read the words aloud. "'Those of you who have workaholic husbands know what I mean when I say sometimes I feel like a single parent.' A rather candid statement."

Miranda wagged a finger at the screen. "More evidence for our cheating theory."

"But it doesn't confirm it."

"No. But it does mean their marriage was less than Heaven-made. They had problems."

"Every married couple does."

She let out a sigh. He was playing devil's advocate, but he was right. They had certainly had their share of rough spots. With all their ups and downs, she wondered what she might have written in a blog if she'd kept one since they met.

And if there had been foul play in this case, they needed something solid to prove it. "Okay, what have you got so far?"

Parker rolled his chair back and adjusted it to face her. "I spoke to Prescott's personal physician."

"On Sunday?"

"He was working in the ER of the hospital near the Prescott home and I caught him between patients."

"Lucky break." He must have done that while she'd had the earphones on, listening to videos.

"The doctor confirms Prescott broke his toe six months ago, and he prescribed the oxycodone. I was able to access pharmacy records. The prescription was refilled once."

That must have been the bottle she'd seen in the medicine cabinet. "So Prescott took the pills for a month?"

"They were used in some way."

Miranda wondered what that way might be. And exactly how Parker had accessed those confidential records. Probably with a method that wouldn't be admissible in court.

She thought a moment. "Maybe Prescott became addicted."

"It's possible."

Templeton appeared in the cube opening. "Kadera just called and said the Medical Examiner confirmed Prescott had a fractured little toe that looked to be less than a year old."

"That matches my findings," Parker said. Then he repeated what he'd told Miranda.

"So there might be a month's prescription of oxycodone floating around somewhere."

Maybe in Prescott's blood stream. Though it wouldn't be floating there anymore.

Parker was skeptical. "We haven't confirmed that Prescott took those pills."

"True. Jane said he hadn't taken many of them."

Templeton thought a moment. "Six months ago. Isn't that when Jane said La Stella showed up on her doorstep?"

"Yeah. Maybe she came to check up on him."

Parker considered the idea. "It usually takes about six weeks for such an injury to heal. Prescott wouldn't be walking from the train station to his office during that time."

"So did Stella come over to the house to find out how her sweetie was doing?" Like Kadera had said. Brazen.

But nobody could answer that question. Yet.

Templeton turned to Miranda. "What about you?"

Miranda told her what she'd found on Jane's mommy blog.

Templeton leaned over to get a look at Miranda's screen, her lips moving as she read. "So she felt like a single parent."

Miranda saw compassion in Templeton's eyes. She actually was a single parent.

"When did she write that?"

Miranda scrolled up to the date on the post. "A couple of years before the toe incident."

Templeton was silent. Then she looked at her cell phone. "It's almost four-thirty, we're stymied, and it's Sunday. There's not much more we can do tonight, but I'd like to visit Prescott's employer first thing in the morning and see what his coworkers can tell us about him. Are you two up for that?"

Miranda looked at Parker. After this morning, she'd let him make the decision.

"Let's discuss that later," he said to her. He turned to Templeton. "If you don't mind."

"No problem. Let me know."

"Will do." Miranda shut down the computer.

Parker did the same.

Just as the screens went black and Miranda started to reach for her coat, one of the uniforms came up to Templeton.

"Excuse me, Detective."

"What is it, Brown?"

"There's someone here from last night wanting to speak to you."

"Who is it?"

"Name's Donahue. He says he has a confession to make. I put him in room C."

"I'll be right there." She turned to Miranda. "You two want to come?"

Confession? Were they going to wrap this case up tonight?

Now Parker's eyes glowed with interest.

Miranda put her coat back on the hook. "Wouldn't miss it for the world."

CHAPTER TWENTY

Miranda stepped into the interrogation room and eyed the dull green paint on the walls, the camera in the corner of the ceiling, and the sullen man sitting at the plain cafeteria table.

Parker held out a chair, like she was going to have dinner with the guy, and without comment she settled into it and waited for him to do the same for Templeton.

He remained standing as Donahue stared at her.

"Miranda Steele? What are you doing here?"

"Hello, Dwight. My husband and I are helping the police."

"That's right. Someone said last night you'd become a private investigator."

"Yes. We both are."

He shook his head. "I asked to speak to the police."

"That would be me. Detective Templeton." Templeton held out a hand.

Timidly, Donahue shook it. "Yes. I remember you from last night."

"Ms. Steele and Mr. Parker are assisting us in the investigation," Templeton explained.

He nodded and eyed Miranda as if he didn't care for the idea.

Miranda studied the man. He was her own age, but he had a youthful round face with smooth unblemished skin, unlike the pimples she remembered dotting his cheeks in high school. He might have gone to a dermatologist. Or stopped drinking sodas. His dark hair was parted down the side in a standard business look. His glasses and jeans and T-shirt were designer.

Altogether he was pretty good looking now.

She recalled wondering what Donahue and Prescott were talking about last night. Time to find out.

"Jane told me you work for NASA."

Donahue shifted his weight as if he were uncomfortable. "Yes. I help design software for testing flight systems inside and outside of the atmosphere."

"Sounds interesting."

He frowned at her. "It's very fulfilling."

"And you work in Florida?"

"That's right."

"Long way to come for a high school reunion."

"I—I wanted to see everyone. Touch base with my old friends."

Miranda sat back with a smirk. "Like Quinton Prescott?"

Donahue looked down at the table. Now he squirmed in his seat the way he did when Prescott used to tease him in Biology class.

"Of course, Quinton and I were never close. Frankly, I was shocked when he contacted me over social media a few months ago."

Miranda glanced at Parker. This was news.

"What did he say to you on social media, Mr. Donahue?" Parker asked.

The engineer lifted his head and took a breath as he turned to Parker, looking grateful for the modicum of respect. "At first it was just the normal chit-chat you have with people online. You know, old times in high school, our kids, how time has flown. That sort of thing. Then he started pressing me to come to the reunion."

"What did you tell him?"

"At first I made excuses. It was a bad time of the year, I had a big project at work. I didn't really want to see him again. Then he said he had something important to ask me, and he had to do it in person. I was curious, so I made arrangements to go."

Miranda thought of the time Prescott sprayed Donahue with silly string in the lunchroom, and everyone laughed at him. Could a grudge have been brewing in Donahue for nineteen years? A grudge big enough to make the geek kill the prom king?

Hanging him by his tie did have the air of a gruesome sort of high school prank.

"What did Prescott ask you that was so important?" Templeton said.

Donahue put his hands on the table and stared at the green wall as if the answer was written there. "He started talking about his job at Sikora and Vogel. He was a partner, had come up in the ranks pretty fast. He said he was responsible for bringing in a large percentage of the firm's business. I thought he was going to press me for NASA contacts to sell services to." He stared down at his hands again.

Miranda leaned forward. "And what did he say?"

Donahue glared at her with a bewildered expression. "He asked me for a job."

A job? "Why would he do that?"

"He said the pressure was getting to him at Sikora and Vogel. Said he wanted to take time off and have a change of scenery."

"And what did you tell him?"

"I told him he'd have to contact the General Counsel's office. I said I'd give him a reference, but I didn't really know anyone there."

"You brushed him off."

"I didn't know what else I could do for him."

Templeton was getting impatient. "Mr. Donahue. The officer told me you had a confession to make."

"I did. I do."

"Well? What is it?"

Donahue drew in a slow breath. "Later on when everyone was dancing, I went out to the terrace to get some air. I saw Quinton on one of the couches. He asked me to sit down and have a drink with him. I said I'd had enough. I didn't sit down, so he came over to me. We were at the banister looking out at the city."

Miranda recalled seeing them together when she and Parker were making out on the terrace.

"And?"

"And, he apologized for pressing me so hard earlier and for dragging me to Chicago and away from my family. I think he did, anyway."

"You think?"

"Quinton was drinking pretty heavily. He was tossing back dry martinis like they were going out of style. He was slurring his words, but I'm fairly sure that's what he said." He stared at the green wall again as if he were solving a math problem written there.

Templeton cleared her throat. "We're waiting, Mr. Donahue."

Donahue ran a hand over his face. "I could tell he was really upset about something. He kept mumbling about all the pressure he was under and how he couldn't please everybody. I asked him if he was all right. He said he was, except for woman trouble."

Miranda's brows shot up. "What do you think he meant by that?"

"I wasn't sure. Then he asked me if I knew what it felt like to be stalked."

Miranda glanced at Parker. "Stalked? Are you sure you heard him clearly?"

"That part was loud and clear."

"What did you say to him?"

"I just wanted to get away from him at that point. I told him he should go inside, get some coffee, and sober up a bit."

"And did he?"

Donahue shook his head. "He just laughed. It reminded me of the way he used to laugh at me in school. I thought, whatever, man."

"And you went back inside."

"I wanted to leave, but I went to the men's room first. Then I heard the screaming and came back in." Donahue's eyes began to fill with tears.

But he still hadn't answered the question. Miranda leaned in close and put a hand on his wrist. "What's your confession, Dwight?"

He looked up at her, the tears starting to flow down his cheeks. "Isn't it obvious? Quinton was in such a bad way. I should have stayed with him. I should have made him come inside and get that coffee. If I had, he'd still be alive. This is all my fault."

Then he put his head on the table and sobbed.

CHAPTER TWENTY-ONE

"It wasn't his fault." Miranda believed him. Every word. Donahue might be a geek, but he wasn't a liar.

They'd spent an hour trying to calm him down and convince him he wasn't responsible for what happened to Prescott before sending him back to his hotel.

As Miranda stepped outside and into the chilly night air of the parking lot, she wasn't sure their talking had done much good.

"I believe him." Templeton's breath was visible as she let out a tired sigh.

Parker stopped on the sidewalk. "Which leads us back to suicide."

It sure did.

Templeton scanned the squad cars parked in the long aisles of the lot. "I'm going ahead as planned." She turned to Miranda. "Are you still up for the law firm tomorrow?"

"Yeah. I mean, what do you think?" Miranda turned to Parker. He'd said he'd wanted to discuss it. She didn't want to push him into it.

She was surprised when Parker nodded without hesitation. "We can do that."

Suddenly a smallish woman in a red coat came around the corner of the building, and hurried up the sidewalk to Templeton.

Reaching the detective, she jammed a microphone into her face. "Did you say the Quinton Prescott incident at the Royal Rose Hotel was suicide?"

Before Templeton could answer, a man with a camera and another woman holding a light jogged over from the lot's entrance.

Miranda stepped off the sidewalk and peeked around the corner.

A local news truck sat at the curb right in front of the No Parking sign.

Good grief.

Templeton seemed a little rattled, but she pulled herself together. "I can tell you we haven't determined anything definite yet," she said to the woman in the red coat.

"And you are—?"

"Detective Templeton of the Larrabee office." She gestured to the building behind her, in case it wasn't obvious.

"Are you in charge of the investigation?"

Templeton looked like she'd rather not say, but she nodded. "I am."

"Detective, when will you know something definite about the case?"

As Templeton paused for a reply, Miranda remembered what Demarco said about the pressure to close this case fast. And that leading this investigation was something of a test for Templeton.

"Soon, I hope," Templeton said at last. "This is an ongoing investigation and we're utilizing all available resources to determine exactly what occurred in this incident."

Now that was some good cop doublespeak.

"And is that Miranda Steele and Wade Parker with you?"

The woman had done her homework.

Without waiting for a reply, the reporter stuck the microphone into Miranda's face. "What's your opinion, Ms. Steele?"

That you're a bitch, Miranda thought. The last thing she wanted was to be on television again.

But she drew in air and put on her best Parker imitation. "The police are doing a fine job in this matter."

"Then why have you and your husband been called in?"

"It always helps to have another set of eyes or two," Miranda said as if she were talking about buying real estate.

Like a hungry dog with a bone, the reporter wouldn't let it go. "Meaning things aren't going well? Someone on the hotel staff told us Mr. Prescott was murdered."

She was really digging for a story. A sensational one.

Parker couldn't hold back his protective instincts any longer. He stepped between Miranda and the reporter. "As Detective Templeton has said, nothing has been determined definitely yet. And as a member of the press, I'm sure you would never broadcast conjecture. Sergeant Demarco will contact the media when he's ready to call a press conference."

"And when will that be?"

Man, she was persistent. Plus she was eyeing Parker the way most women did.

Miranda wanted to smack her.

"Perhaps sooner than you think. Now if you'll excuse us." Parker took both Miranda and Templeton by the elbow and led them over to the police Tahoe.

The reporter and her camera crew stood on the sidewalk for a moment, summing things up, then disappeared back around the corner.

The news hounds had a bone to gnaw on, though Miranda wasn't sure Demarco would like the bit about the press conference.

As they reached the Tahoe's driver side, Templeton let out a breath of relief. "Thanks, Mr. Parker."

"You're welcome, Detective."

"I'll text you the address of Prescott's law firm. We've got a nine o'clock with Lawrence Vogel in the morning."

"We'll be there."

They waited for Templeton to get into her car, then made their way to the rented Jaguar. They got inside and followed her to the street. The TV truck was gone, thank goodness. But the damage had already been done.

Quinton Prescott's death would be reported as a possible murder.

CHAPTER TWENTY-TWO

Back at the hotel, Parker insisted on stopping in one of the restaurants for a light dinner.

They were serving Asian fare, so he ordered a Shanghai style salad, wonton soup with bok choy, scallions, and ginger, crispy Thai spring rolls, and oolong tea. Every bite and sip was delicious, but even though the meal was just appetizers, when she finished, Miranda was stuffed.

So much for Parker's idea of "light."

Hoping for an early night, she rode up the elevator on Parker's arm and headed for their suite. She was already yawning as she stepped into the bedroom.

"So now we've confirmed Prescott was depressed, after all," she said, pulling on her sleep shirt.

"We've confirmed he gave that impression to one person." Unbuttoning his shirt at the closet, Parker sounded wary. "This case may go cold rather quickly."

"It could." She brushed at her hair with her fingers.

And what would they do then? Maybe come back in four of five months? If there was a new development. But she and Parker could be dancing their way across Europe by then.

She'd have to let this thing go at some point.

She took the accent pillows off the bed and tossed them onto the chaise lounge chair. "We do know Prescott was intoxicated and had oxycodone in his bloodstream."

"And because of that, it would have been difficult for him to tie the knot in his tie."

She lay down on the fluffy mattress and thought about that. "But is suicide impossible? Prescott's brain was blitzed. Maybe he thought he was tying his shoe and then slipping into bed as he pulled himself over the banister."

Parker scowled as he sat down on the end of the bed. "There was the other comment Donahue made."

She knew what he meant. "That Prescott thought he was being stalked."

"To be precise, he asked Donahue if he knew what it was like to be stalked."

Parker had a little experience in that realm.

He grabbed the remote and turned on the big screen TV on the wall.

"What are you doing?"

"I just want to see if—ah, there it is."

A woman's face appeared on the screen. A news reporter.

Miranda hopped out of bed and came closer to the screen for a better view.

Yep. It was the same woman who'd snagged them for her interview earlier that night.

Wearing the same red coat, she stood on the sidewalk in front of the fancy glass doors of a hotel lobby.

"A freak accident. That's what some are calling the death of a prominent Chicago attorney here at the Royal Rose Hotel." She gestured behind her. "We've learned that Quinton Preston fell to his death last night on the rooftop terrace twenty stories above."

The camera panned up the side of the tall building, but you couldn't really see the terrace.

Fell? In a manner of speaking. Miranda guessed the police hadn't released the goriest details yet.

"Earlier this evening, I spoke to the police investigators in charge of the case."

Now the image switched to Templeton's face as she was saying what she'd told the reporter a few hours ago. "This is an ongoing investigation, and we're utilizing all available resources to determine exactly what occurred in this incident."

"And we also have two private investigators involved. It seems Miranda Steele and Wade Parker of the Parker Investigative Agency in Atlanta are assisting authorities here."

Miranda saw herself scowling down at the reporter's microphone. "The police are doing a fine job in this matter."

Parker's handsome face came on the screen. He always looked good on camera. "Nothing has been determined definitely yet."

Back to the reporter. "We're staying on top of this story and will be the first to bring you any updates...."

Miranda bared her teeth at the TV. "Oh, good Lord. Turn that off."

"I've seen enough." Parker raised the remote, then paused. "What do we have here?"

The story ended, and another familiar face appeared on the screen. Luscious black hair, piercing blue eyes, tight green dress, tempting smile.

A sultry voice filled the room. "Passing light showers in tonight's forecast with cool breezes off the Lake, but a warmer day tomorrow. More after the break."

Stella La Stella. The weather girl.

Parker shut off the TV, but Miranda stared at the screen.

"What are you thinking, Miranda?"

"I'm thinking that Donahue said Prescott mentioned 'woman trouble'." she cringed at the term, but wondered if she knew who he'd meant.

"And you think he was talking about Stella?"

She pulled down the covers again and climbed back into bed. "I guess I'm pretty transparent."

"Not at all." Parker came to his side of the bed and got in beside her. "Prescott may have been talking about Jane."

She thought about that. "Yeah. Maybe she complained about his being away from home so much, and he didn't like it."

"She might have."

"Maybe she was getting ready to ask him for a divorce."

"Possible, but still conjecture."

It was all they had. Feeling frustrated, she gave her pillow a sock, lay down and closed her eyes. "Maybe we'll learn something at the law firm tomorrow."

"Perhaps."

"In my head I just keep seeing Stella running in from the terrace and screaming for help."

"She was distraught."

"Or was it an act?"

Parker slipped an arm around her. "Do you think she killed Prescott?"

Miranda nestled into his shoulder and thought a moment. "I don't know. She wasn't out on the terrace very long. If she tied that tie to the banister and pushed him over, she'd have to work fast. Even if she'd managed to do it, there wasn't enough time for Prescott to expire before you got to him and pulled him back over. The ME's report said five to ten minutes. All that didn't take that long."

"That's true."

Her eyes popped open. "Wait a minute."

"What is it?"

"Before all that happened, Jane was at the podium going on and on about her committee. Do you remember?"

Parker nodded. "She was thanking them effusively for their help with the reunion. You wanted her to hurry and announce the contest winner."

"Right. But Stella wasn't there right away. She came up to the podium when Jane called her." She poked at his chest with her finger.

He grabbed her finger and kissed it. "She said she had been in the ladies room."

And her nose was red. "What if she stopped off at the terrace before she went there? That would be enough time to get it done."

"It would have been more than ten minutes."

"So we have means, motive, and opportunity."

"We have conjectured means, motive, and opportunity."

"Still, it's something."

"Not enough for even the most lenient DA."

He was right. "We'll find out more tomorrow." Maybe.

With a sigh, she put her head down on Parker's shoulder again and closed her eyes.

And with visions of a distraught Stella La Stella arguing with a drunken Quinton Prescott on the terrace twenty stories above Michigan Avenue, she drifted off to sleep.

CHAPTER TWENTY-THREE

The next morning began with eggs Benedict and strong hot coffee in the living room of the suite. Then quick showers and pulling on the crisp fresh business suits Parker had sent out to be cleaned.

A dark gray one-button blazer and matching slacks for her, a dark blue wool blend tailored suit with white shirt and silver tie for him.

Back in the cabin in Georgia, they had packed so fast, out of force of habit, Miranda had grabbed several business suits. Parker had done the same, but he'd probably intended to wear them to restaurants.

Then it was back in the Jag for a two-block ride to the law firm on South Wacker in bumper-to-bumper city traffic that made Miranda understand why Prescott took the train to work every day.

They met Templeton in the majestic black marble lobby and rode up the elevator to the forty-seventh floor.

The doors opened, and they crossed a floor made to look like textured oak, but was really cork. To cut down on the noise, Miranda imagined.

In a large space with dazzling paintings of fuzzy pastel objects on the walls, they approached a sweeping red cedar receptionist desk where a woman as polished as its chrome accents sat. Dressed in a dark gray sweater, with her sleek champagne blond hair parted down the middle and tucked behind ears where silver leaf shapes sparkled, she turned to them with a robotic half smile.

"May I help you?"

She reminded Miranda a little of Cybil at the Agency.

Templeton held out the ID on her lanyard. "I'm Detective Templeton with the Chicago PD, and this is Miranda Steele and Wade Parker. We're here to see Mr. Lawrence Vogel."

"Do you have an appointment?"

"Yes, we do."

Except for the typical gape at Parker, the woman acted as if the police came to her desk every day. "One moment, please."

She turned away, pressed a button, spoke into her headset, and turned back with a smile. "Someone will be with you in a moment."

They moved to a waiting area, sat down in some oddly shaped bright teal chairs and stared at the nondescript paintings.

After about fifteen minutes, a young woman came up to them. She was dressed in a stiff black suit and had her ash blond hair pulled back at the nape of her neck.

She held out a hand, and they each shook with her. "I'm Helen King, Mr. Vogel's aide," she said in a no nonsense tone. "Please follow me."

She led them down a short hall and through a large open space lined with twenty-foot high windows revealing breath-taking views of the city. They made a sharp turn and moved through another corridor, passing offices with glass walls where lawyers were meeting with clients or talking on the phone, or working at laptops.

Everything here was bright and big.

Finally, they reached the end of the hall and followed Helen King into a monstrous corner office with pale brick walls and huge windows with more heart-stopping views of the surrounding buildings.

"Please have a seat," the aide said.

The desk was a flat drawer-less oval with spindly, spider like chrome legs, and the guest chairs were just as minimalist and didn't look very comfortable, but they sat anyway.

"I apologize for Mr. Vogel's delay. He's stuck in traffic, but he'll be here shortly. Can I get you anything to drink?"

"No, thank you," Parker said.

Miranda shook her head.

Templeton raised a finger. "I'll take a coffee. Cream and sugar."

"Very good. I'll be right back."

When the aide had left, she turned to them. "I just want to make sure she comes back."

The coffee didn't come, but it was only about another five minutes before Lawrence Vogel walked through the door.

"I am so sorry I've kept you waiting. Please don't get up."

He was a tall, elegant looking man with a shock of white wavy hair and thick gray brows. In a tailored pinstripe suit and red silk tie, he looked like the top partner in the top Chicago law firm. A man used to having things go his way.

He shook hands with everyone, they introduced themselves, and then he took a seat behind the sparse desk and looked directly at Templeton. "I suppose this is about what happened to Quinton over the weekend?"

"Yes, Mr. Vogel, it is. I hope you don't mind if we ask you a few questions."

"Please call me Lawrence." He ran a hand through his hair. "I just heard the news this morning. I was in Wisconsin on a fishing trip with my son all weekend. I must say, I'm still in shock. I suppose I'm going to have to hold a meeting and break the news to the staff."

That should be fun.

Miranda stole a glance at Parker. His face was expressionless, but she could tell he was wondering how much information they were going to get about Prescott from freshly stunned coworkers. Though some of them may have seen the story on the news.

Templeton leaned forward. "Mr. Vogel, Lawrence, what kind of worker was Mr. Prescott?"

Vogel seemed surprised by the question. "Quinton? One of the best. Bright, enthusiastic, ambitious. He put in long hours, was very dedicated to the job."

Templeton took a note in her book.

"Did he ever get down about anything?" Miranda asked.

"Down? No. He was a consummate optimist. Always smiling and joking."

That didn't match with what Donahue told them last night. Maybe Prescott was hiding a dark side.

Templeton continued. "We understand he was under a good deal of pressure here at work."

"Being a partner in any law firm comes with pressure. But as I said, Quinton was one of our best. He brought in a great deal of business and booked a lot of billable hours. And he had fun with it. He loved his work."

So much so, he was looking for another job in Florida.

Parker leaned back in his chair. "How closely did you work with Mr. Prescott, Lawrence?"

Vogel had to think a minute for that one. "We met once a week to go over his progress with various clients. Occasionally we went out for drinks together."

Translation. Not that closely.

"Did he seem upset about anything lately? Perhaps a little moody?"

"Quinton? No, not at all. He was always in a good mood. He was working on the Carson deal with Theo Foster. He was excited he was getting close to an agreement." Vogel stared out the window as if he were lost. "I suppose I'll have to call Theo and tell him what happened."

Sounded to Miranda like Quinton Prescott was good at fooling his boss.

Templeton cleared her throat. "We'd like to speak to some of your employees, if we may."

Vogel frowned. "Oh?"

"Those who worked closely with him."

"Yes. I understand. Helen can get you a list of those names. Let me call that meeting and tell them what happened first." He narrowed his eyes at Templeton. "I understand it was some sort of bizarre accident at his high school reunion?"

Templeton met his gaze without batting an eye. "We're still investigating the circumstances. But yes, that's what happened."

CHAPTER TWENTY-FOUR

The meeting was held in one of the huge open areas of the office.

As the rain Stella La Stella had predicted doused the panes of the tall windows, about a hundred or so employees gathered in the middle of the floor.

Vogel stepped onto a raised platform, and in a deep booming voice, told the firm their colleague was gone.

There was a stunned silence, then a gasp, then people near the back began to sob.

"The police are here and will want to speak to some of you," Vogel told them. "But after they dismiss you, feel free to take the rest of the day."

Helen found an empty room, and Miranda and Parker and Templeton spent the next four hours interviewing senior partners, junior partners, associates, law clerks, and members of the clerical staff.

Everyone said basically the same thing Vogel had. Quinton Prescott was a great guy. A good lawyer, hardworking, productive, and friendly. The word "optimistic" came up several times.

So why was he looking for a new job? Why was he drinking so hard at the reunion? Why did he seem paranoid and depressed? And why was there oxycodone in his bloodstream?

Or had Dwight Donahue lied last night?

"I think it's time to break for some lunch," Parker said, rising from the cushioned office chair that matched the ones Miranda and Templeton were sitting in.

Bunched together on the far side of a fancy conference table, they must have looked like some kind of tribunal.

Miranda glanced at her phone. It was after two-thirty. "Good idea."

"I'm game." Templeton rose and looked out the tall window where the skyscrapers were looming. "Rain's stopped."

They shuffled around the table, and Parker had just opened the door for the ladies when a meek looking woman appeared in the opening, her hand raised as if about to knock.

The woman was on the short side. Her straight dark hair and bangs that brushed the tops of her black rimmed glasses fringed a round curious face. She had on a wool gray suit that looked uncomfortable and her feet were packed into a pair of gray pumps.

She looked scared.

"Is Detective Templeton here?" she asked in a semi-hoarse voice.

"Why, yes. She's right here." Parker gestured behind him.

"How can I help you?" Templeton said.

The woman entered the room with mincing steps and clasped her hands in front of her chest, as if she were begging for an audience with a queen. "My name is Ivy Flores. I'm a paralegal in the Tax department. I heard you were asking questions about Mr. Prescott."

Templeton looked at Miranda. Miranda turned to the woman. "Do you have something to tell us?"

"I think so."

They could postpone the late lunch if this was good.

"Why don't we all sit down and discuss it?" Parker said, his deep Southern voice oozing his usual charm.

The corner of the woman's mouth turned up, then down again. "I don't want to interrupt if you're taking a break."

"Not at all." Parker closed the door, moved back to the table, and held out a chair opposite the other three for Ms. Flores.

Miranda stole a glance at him. He was thinking what she was. This could be the one. Or Ms. Flores could be here to tell them how optimistic Prescott was, so she could leave and go home.

They had to go through the motions to find out.

Miranda went around the table and took a seat while Templeton settled in next to her, and Parker took the chair next to Flores.

Good move, Miranda thought. Make her more relaxed.

Templeton opened her notebook and clicked her pen. "What do you have to say, Ms. Flores?"

Flores eyed Templeton's pen. "Um, I heard you were asking if Mr. Prescott had any, uh—personal problems."

The office must be buzzing with gossip about their interviews.

Templeton gave Miranda a nod, indicating for her to take this one.

She turned to Flores. "Do you have something to say about Mr. Prescott's personal problems?"

The woman blinked at her, then glanced at Templeton's pen again. "I—is this confidential? I could lose my job."

Miranda sat back and folded her hands. That was up to Templeton. She couldn't promise anything.

"We can keep your identity confidential." Templeton closed her notebook and put down her pen, and Miranda let out a breath she didn't realize she was holding.

"What do you have to say to us, Ivy?" Parker's voice was as gentle as a lapping brook. He knew how to get information out of people.

Ivy Flores looked down at her hands which were now in her lap, still clasped. "It's just that—"

"Yes?"

She drew in a breath. "Quinton and I used to talk."

She had been on a first name basis with him, though that seemed to be the norm here. "What did you talk about?"

Ivy hugged herself and looked away. "Personal things."

Miranda waited.

"I worked with him on a couple of projects about three years ago, and we had a lot of long nights together. We ate a lot of Chinese takeout together." She laughed sadly, then cleared her throat.

"And?" Parker prompted.

"I really don't know how it happened, but we started to talk about our private lives. He told me he had a lot of problems with his wife." She gazed out the window.

Miranda shifted her weight. "What kind of problems?"

"He said she didn't understand him. She used to be part of his world, but she wasn't any more. She used to work here as a paralegal."

Jane had mentioned she got a job at a law firm, but hadn't said it was Prescott's. That must have been how they'd reconnected after high school. "What else did he tell you?"

"It was during the Pickrell deal. It involved the acquisition of a multibillion dollar company. Really stressful. I remember one night Quinton was sitting in a chair in the conference room where we'd spread out all the documents. He was rocking back and forth, chewing on his moo shu pork. And he told me—"

No one said a word as Ivy took a breath.

"He told me he was having an affair with Emma Jenkins."

Templeton opened her notebook and turned the pages while Miranda looked over her shoulder.

"I believe she's a junior partner in Capital Markets." Parker didn't need notes.

"She is now," Ivy said. "Back then she was an associate. She was on Quinton's team."

Sticky. And worthy of dismissal if either of them were discovered. No wonder this woman was nervous.

Miranda leaned forward and folded her hands on the table. "What does that have to do with Mr. Prescott's recent problems?"

"Well, you see, Emma was just the first."

Okay. "Can you elaborate?"

"I think it was two, maybe three months later, one night when we were working on another case, I asked about Emma and he said, 'Oh, I'm done with her.' I thought that wasn't a very nice way of putting it, but I asked him if he'd gotten on better terms with his wife. He said no, she still was in another world. And then he said he was dating Nicole Clark."

Before Templeton could turn a page in her notebook, Ivy added, "She's a clerk in Finance and Lending. She's still there."

Miranda recalled speaking with the statuesque blonde and wondering why she didn't seem as upset over the news about Prescott as some of the others.

"And then about four months went by, and Quinton tells me he's dumped Nicole and now he's with Elenor Gonzalez in Private Equity."

Miranda watched Parker's jaw twitch. He hated cheaters as much as she did. Poor Jane. Miranda wondered how much she knew about this. Maybe nothing. Isn't the wife always the last to know?

Gently, Parker patted the woman's hand. "It sounds like there were others, Ivy."

"There were, but I didn't know them. After that, Quinton decided to go outside the office. I guess he got tired of the risk."

Miranda cleared her throat. "Do you think any of these women might have planned to kill him?"

Ivy nearly laughed. "I think most everyone he had affairs with wanted to kill him. It wasn't just casual sex. Each of his affairs went on for weeks. Quinton was a charmer. He'd wine and dine them. Give them flowers. Find out what they liked most and give them gifts they'd really appreciate. He'd make them fall in love with him. Then, after a month or two, he'd dump them."

Miranda felt a little sick. She didn't remember Prescott being that much of a jerk in high school. "Did he say why?"

The woman's shoulders bunched under her gray suit. "He'd just lose interest. He was so self absorbed. I asked him if he was in love with any of them, and he said no. He told me he was looking for what he felt in high school when girls used to worship him. He also told me once he thought he was a sex addict." She let out a snort. "I think he was a narcissist."

What a creep he'd turned out to be. And yet this woman kept up a friendship with him.

Miranda leaned forward. "Ivy, did you have an affair with Quinton Prescott?"

"Me?" Her eyes fluttered and her cheeks turned red in embarrassment. "Oh, no. I wasn't his type. He had, um, high standards. He only wanted tall women in good shape."

Ivy definitely wasn't a fashion model. Her looks were no more than average. Maybe she was jealous. Maybe she knew more than she thought.

"Do you know who Prescott was dating currently?"

"Not really. He stopped telling me the names when he went outside the office. And we haven't worked together on any projects for a year or so. But we'd have lunch together every once in a while. The last time was back before the holidays. Novemberish. He didn't confide in me like he used to, but he dropped hints. I think he was definitely seeing someone around that time. I think he'd been seeing her for a while. Several months. Seemed like it had lasted longer than most."

Miranda's pulse sped up. She glanced at Parker.

"And was he about to break up with her?" he prompted.

Ivy frowned as if she had to think about the answer. "He didn't tell me so directly, but I thought he was."

"What gave you that impression?"

"Well, it was time for it. The longest he ever stayed with anyone before was four months. But there was something bothering him about this one."

"What was it?"

"Quinton was kind of irritable, not at all like himself. He looked like he hadn't been sleeping well." Ivy fidgeted in her chair, looked down at her hands again. "Don't ask me how I know this. It was mostly intuition. But I think this one was threatening to tell his wife."

Could that have been Stella?

Miranda sat back and resisted the urge to do a fist pump. "Where did Prescott take you to lunch?"

"We always went to The Sapphire Grille. It was his favorite place. It's about a three-minute walk from here."

CHAPTER TWENTY-FIVE

When they stepped outside and onto the sidewalk, the cold wind nearly took Miranda's breath.

She pulled her coat around her. "So much for the forecast of warmer temperatures."

Templeton shoved her hands into her pockets. "You can never predict Chicago weather this time of year."

About as fickle as Atlanta's.

"I would offer to get the car for you ladies," Parker said, "but the parking garage is near the restaurant. It will take less time to walk."

"We can handle a little wind." Miranda turned and led the way up the sidewalk, through the glass office towers and skyscrapers looming on either side, past the noisy traffic, until she reached a narrow alleyway.

She peered down it.

Near the far end where the alley met the next road, she saw a row of bicycles and motorcycles parked along a windowless metal wall. On the other side trucks delivered goods to the back of stores.

"There it is." Templeton pointed to a bright red-and-white sign over the establishment on the corner.

The Sapphire Grille. Must be it.

Parker opened the door for them. "Let's see what the fare is like."

An unsmiling hostess greeted them stiffly and led them to a corner table.

Parker held out a chair first for Templeton, then for Miranda.

Templeton's cheeks turned red as she sat down.

The snippy hostess handed them menus. "We're serving dinner now," she said and disappeared.

"Nice spot," Templeton said sincerely, ignoring the hostess's attitude.

"Yeah." Miranda sized the place up.

The décor was old brick with rustic wooden doors and circular wrought iron candle lights that gave the place a medieval flare.

From the corner, they had a good view of the rest of the room, but there weren't many people here. A party of three sat behind a brick column in the center, and a few business people in tables were along the opposite wall.

"See anyone from Prescott's firm in here?" she said.

Templeton scanned the floor. "No one I recognize, but it's past lunch time."

As the hostess had reminded them. "I wonder if Prescott took any of his lovers here."

Just then Templeton sucked in her breath. Who had she seen? Miranda turned her head and saw she'd just opened the menu.

She did the same. Wow. The place was pricey.

Parker smiled smoothly. "The Agency will pick up the tab."

Templeton shook her head. "I can't let you do that. I have an expense account."

That she'd have to answer for.

"We'll roll the cost of the meal into our fee. This is investigative work, after all. Isn't it?"

It was no use arguing with Parker. Templeton gave in. "Well, okay. But I'll get the tip."

After a while a waitress came over, introduced herself as Cynthia, and took their orders.

Miranda decided to indulge in a plate of seafood fettuccine bathed in a rich sherry cream sauce. Parker selected shrimp risotto with spinach and parmesan. And though she didn't have to, Templeton ordered the cheapest thing on the menu, which was chicken penne with asparagus and broccolini in a white wine sauce.

As they waited for the food, once more Miranda scanned the other guests. She didn't recognize any of them, either. After Ivy Flores's revelation, they had decided they were done for the day, and most of the employees of Sikora and Vogel had gone home. They probably wouldn't learn much here, but since they had to eat, it was worth checking out.

Soon the delicious smelling meals were served.

Miranda had to smile at the expression on Templeton's face as she dug into her dish.

"Oh, man. This is good," she said, closing her eyes as she savored the flavorful pasta.

Miranda watched Parker's eyes twinkle and remembered the first time he'd bought her a pricey meal. She'd reacted about the same. Now he had her thoroughly spoiled.

Miranda concentrated on the food for the next several minutes. But as she finished, she began to mull over what Ivy Flores had told them.

Templeton took out her notebook and scanned it. "We talked to all three of the women Ivy mentioned, and all of them said they didn't know Prescott well."

"They wouldn't admit they were having an affair with him. Why risk your job for someone who's dead?" Miranda popped the last bite of fettuccine into her mouth.

"Good point." Templeton's shoulders sank as she put her notebook back in her purse and pushed her plate away.

Parker had already finished his dish. He was on his phone.

"What are you doing?" Miranda asked.

"Looking at the Sikora and Vogel website. They have photos of all their employees, listed by division."

Miranda leaned forward. "Let me see that."

She took the phone and stared down at Prescott's grinning face. *Quinton Prescott, Partner, Corporate.* Dressed in a gray suit and red tie, he looked ready to take on any multimillion dollar deal. His tight blond curls were neatly trimmed, and his dimples made him look authoritative instead of youthful.

But there was a strange glint in his blue eyes. A kind of meanness. Or maybe it was desperation.

Who was after you, Prescott? Was it who I think it was?

"A different woman every three or four months for three years," Templeton murmured in disbelief.

"That we know of," Parker added with a low growl.

"He could have gone through a dozen." Miranda tapped her fingers on the table. Then she turned to Templeton. "Do you have Prescott's phone records?"

Templeton swallowed the mouthful of soda she'd just gulped. "Prescott had recently cleared his call and text history, but Kadera's supposed to be getting the records from his cell carrier. I'll text him." She pulled out her phone and tapped out a message. Then she leaned over to have a look at Prescott's photo. "I wonder if that's recent. Maybe they have some from previous years. They might show a pattern that indicates, I don't know. Mental deterioration?"

Miranda held up a finger. "I've got a better idea."

Just then Cynthia returned and began removing the empty plates.

"Excuse me," Miranda said to her. "I'm wondering if this gentleman is one of your regular guests."

She held up Parker's phone.

Her arms full of platters, the woman peered down at the screen and smiled instantly. "Why, yes. That's Quinton Prescott. He works at Sikora and Vogel down the street."

She knew him by name. And where he worked.

"So he comes here often?"

"Oh, yes. He's in here once or twice a week, at least."

"For lunch?"

"Mostly. I think he comes in for dinner, too, but that's not my shift."

Interesting. "Does he dine alone?"

"Sometimes. Usually he's with a client or a party. They're always discussing complicated financial affairs. Venture capital, corporate restructuring. I'm going to business school at night, so I'm familiar with some of the terms."

Miranda grinned. "Good for you. Do you recall whether Mr. Prescott's clients were men or women?"

Cynthia considered the question a moment. "Hmm. I never thought about it before, but when he was with a group it was usually men. When it was just Mr. Prescott and the client, it was usually a woman. Isn't that funny? Are you friends of his?"

Evidently, she was too busy with work and school to watch the news.

Parker took the lead on this one. "Cynthia, I'm sorry to tell you that Mr. Prescott passed away over the weekend."

The young woman's face went pale. "Oh, no. That's terrible."

"Actually, we're with the police and we're investigating the matter," Miranda told her.

"Police? Oh, my. He wasn't involved in something illegal, was he?"

Parker leaned back in his chair. "Not that we know of, We're simply looking for unusual patterns in his behavior of late. Something that indicated depression or that he was troubled over something."

Cynthia's brow creased. "I'm not sure I can help you with that. He always seemed pretty upbeat to me. Come to think of it, I haven't seen him in here for a couple of weeks now. I'm sorry."

"That's all right," Parker smiled kindly. "You've been helpful."

"If you can remember anything else about Mr. Prescott, please feel free to call me." Templeton passed her card across the table.

The woman took the card and read it. "I will." Then she stuffed it into her pocket and put on her happy waitress face. "Is there anything else I can get for you?"

"Just the check," Parker said.

"I'll be right back with it." And Cynthia disappeared.

While they were waiting, Templeton's phone buzzed. She pulled it out and grinned. "Kadera says he just got the phone records and is going through them. There's a lot of data to work through."

Sounded like he could use some help. Miranda gazed across the table at Parker. She'd let him volunteer this time.

He read her meaning and nodded. "Looks like we need to get back to the station and get busy."

She couldn't hold back a smile. He was into this case now.

CHAPTER TWENTY-SIX

The trip to the office was cold and dark and rainy, and the traffic was lousy. It took them over half an hour to travel the two miles back to the Larrabee station.

After they rushed in through the back door to avoid getting wet, they discovered Demarco was waiting for them at the cubes.

He gave Templeton a sour scowl. "Kadera says you've learned our vic was a player."

"Yes, sir."

Templeton must have told Kadera some of the details in her texts to him.

"An affair doesn't prove murder. You know that, don't you, Templeton?"

"Yes, sir."

"At best, it's circumstantial."

"We think it might be more than that," Miranda interrupted.

"Oh?"

"We've got some ideas. We just need to figure out where they lead."

Demarco chewed on his toothpick as he studied her, then eyed Templeton. "I've been fielding calls for the last two hours. After that encounter with the press last night, there's more pressure than ever to close this thing. I wish you had cleared that interview with me, Templeton."

"I'm sorry, sir. The reporter ambushed us when we were leaving last night."

Demarco took the pick out of his mouth and stared down at the carpet as if he was struggling to keep from exploding.

He was a good man, and Miranda knew he didn't want to take his frustration out on Templeton. But the detective's cheeks were already a rosy red.

"All right, then," he said at last. "Get to it. And let me know as soon as you have something."

"Yes, sir."

And so they did.

While Parker went to search out Prescott's financials, Miranda and Templeton divided up the phone records with Kadera. They started with April three years ago and went forward.

It was tedious work. Prescott's job required him to be on the phone a lot. A minimum of three hours a day. Some days there was a flurry of conference calls. Lots of lunch dates. Some texts were brief, others were long and contained attachments of lengthy legal documents.

After about forty minutes, Templeton poked her head up from her cube. "I think I found one from Emma Jenkins."

Miranda hurried over to look at it.

Kadera was right behind her. "What have you got, kid?"

"Right here." She pointed to the screen.

Twelve-thirty is good. I'll meet you at Sapphire.

"I did a reverse lookup on the number and it belongs to Emma Jenkins."

Kadera's lips went back and forth. "Doesn't really prove anything other than they had lunch. What else is there?"

Templeton scrolled through a bunch of calls to corporate vice presidents and CEOs and texts with a lot of contract mumbo jumbo. And then she found another set of messages from the same number.

I had a good time last night.
Me, too. The flowers were sweet.
We need to do it again.

There were heart icons around "do it."

Miranda let out a huff. "That's the type of corporate takeover we're looking for."

Kadera wasn't convinced. "Implies he might have been having an affair with someone three years ago. Someone who wasn't at that reunion party."

"We don't know that." Templeton pulled out a folder. "This is a list Jane gave me of the people who were sent invitations. Those who showed up are checkmarked."

Miranda didn't remember any Emma Jenkins from high school, but she hadn't been there all four years. "Let me look it over. I'll recognize some of those names."

Templeton handed it to her. "I just got access to Prescott's emails. I'll go through those, too."

"Looks like it's going to be a long night."

They went back at it, and after another hour, Miranda thought she was going nuts. If she had to read about one more merger and acquisition, she was going to scream. Or maybe apply for the LSAT.

And then she realized something. The police were too methodical. Why were they going at this backwards? It was the recent stuff they needed.

She dug back into the text records and started at last October. Sure enough, among invitations to Halloween parties, she found the gold.

Hi there, darling. I can't wait to see you tonight.
Are you taking me to our favorite place?

Where else? And then to the moon.

Oh, brother. Miranda's heart was breaking for Jane, and she didn't know how she was going to tell her about all this. And yet, when she did the reverse lookup on the text, she couldn't help but smile.

The number belonged to Stella La Stella.

CHAPTER TWENTY-SEVEN

"It doesn't prove she killed him."

Miranda waved the printout of Stella's and Prescott's messages in Demarco's face. "It gives her motive."

"How?"

Drawing in a frustrated breath, she took in the office Demarco now occupied and wondered if they'd make him a lieutenant soon.

It was a rectangular space alongside the homicide cubes. His desk was another rectangle, this time of faux wood veneer. It was covered with a laptop, half empty coffee cups, papers, and his favorite toothpick holder.

Parker stood alongside matching filing cabinets that lined the opposite end of the room. Templeton and Kadera were near the walls that were hung with the same calendar and wanted posters that were in the cube she and Parker were sharing. The other wall was all window, opening not to the outside, but to the work area so the boss could keep an eye on his people, though it was fitted with blinds for privacy when he preferred it.

Demarco had closed them when everyone had rushed in here.

A little calmer, Miranda laid the printout on Demarco's desk. "Ivy Flores at Sikora and Vogel told us Prescott had many affairs," she explained. "Each one lasted three or four months, then Prescott would break it off and move on to somebody else."

Demarco turned to Parker as if he didn't believe her. "Is that true?"

"It is," Parker said, a steely calm in his voice. "Flores said Prescott would charm the women into falling for him. It was her opinion most of them wanted to kill him."

"And this Flores is—"

"A paralegal we interviewed at Prescott's law firm today, sir," Templeton supplied.

Demarco looked like he had just bit into an onion. "Do you have anyone else to corroborate her claims?"

Templeton's shoulders slumped. "Not yet, sir."

The testimony of the waitress at The Sapphire Grille didn't help much.

"I do have some interesting charges to Prescott's credit card," Parker said.

Demarco's chair creaked as he turned in Parker's direction. "Such as?"

"Expensive dinners at fine restaurants."

"He could have been entertaining clients."

"For some of the charges, yes. But I don't think he was sending flowers to clients or paying for overnight stays at local five-star hotels."

Demarco sat back and rocked in his squeaky chair. "All right. This is something, but it's not nearly enough yet. I've had to field more calls from the higher ups just now. Not to mention the media. They're not letting up. We can't let this case go cold. We have to prove either Prescott did himself in or somebody did it for him."

"Yes, sir. We will."

But probably not tonight. Miranda's stomach was in knots for Templeton.

She almost jumped when an officer knocked on the door.

Demarco frowned with annoyance. "What is it, Brown?"

Brown gave Demarco a steady gaze, as if he was used to his mood swings. "We've got another visitor on the Prescott case."

CHAPTER TWENTY-EIGHT

Miranda stepped into the interview room and saw a small demure looking woman sitting at the table with her back to the wall.

She took a seat across from her, while Templeton and Parker remained standing, and held out a hand. "I'm Miranda Steele, and this is Wade Parker and Detective Shirley Templeton of the Chicago police."

Force of habit made her hand the woman a business card she'd had found stuffed in her pants pocket when she got dressed this morning.

"I know who you are," the woman said sharply as she took the card.

Miranda peered at her.

She had an oblong face, a longish nose, and a narrow chin that was tucked into her neck, so that her dark eyes bore right through Miranda.

"You talked to me Saturday night." Despite the irritation in it, her voice was soft and had a refined lilt to it.

Now Miranda recognized her. "Victoria Winslow."

"That's right."

Piccolo girl. Most Likely to Join the Philharmonic.

She was almost pretty, though the highlights in her dark hair did little to enhance her looks. Neither did her drab shapeless dress and a gray coat. She had always been a dowdy dresser, not that Miranda cared about that sort of thing, but she recalled the other girls used to tease her about her clothes.

She definitely wasn't one of the popular ones. Miranda had always felt sorry for her.

"You were at the reunion."

"Yes."

Templeton sat down next to Miranda and pulled a paper from a folder. Miranda leaned over and saw it was an alphabetized list Kadera had put together.

Templeton scanned the paper. "Your name isn't on the list of those who were interviewed after the party."

"I left early. But I was there. Miranda spoke to me."

"That's correct," Miranda said, feeling cornered.

Templeton took out another paper from the folder. The list Jane had given her. Miranda hadn't found Emma Jenkins on her copy or anyone else they'd interviewed at Prescott's law firm.

Templeton tapped the paper. "Your name's here on the list of people who were sent invitations. There's a checkmark indicating you attended."

Victoria turned her head as Templeton held out the paper, then nodded with a superior air. "That's right."

"Why did you come into the station, Ms. Winslow?"

"I saw the story about what happened to Quinton on the news. I thought I should tell the police what I know about it."

Miranda's stomach went tight.

"And what's that?" Templeton said.

Victoria looked down a moment as if gathering her thoughts. "The night of the party, I saw Quinton on the terrace. He was standing near the banister staring out at the city like he was lost."

Miranda forced disinterest into her voice. "Did you speak to him?"

"No. I didn't have anything to say to him. I didn't know him very well in high school."

She wasn't popular enough to attract Prescott's attention.

"But that's where they said on the news that he was found, right?" Her voice broke a little. "Over the terrace banister?"

"That's correct."

She stared down at the table.

Miranda's heart sank. Victoria Winslow didn't have anything to tell them. She was just trying to do her civic duty and give the interview she should have Saturday night like the other guests had.

Miranda wanted to get back to her desk and follow up on the text she'd found. They should have had Officer Brown talk to this woman.

Templeton's back went straight. "We can't tell you details we haven't released to the press, Ms. Winslow."

Good thought. Victoria must be curious and fishing for news.

"Oh, I understand that. But I'm not finished."

Did she have something to tell them, after all?

Templeton nodded. "Go on."

Victoria inhaled. "As I said, I saw Quinton standing on the terrace at the banister, and after a while, a woman came up to him. They started talking. I'd seen her with him before."

"Where?"

"At the restaurant where I work. It was several months back, but I'm sure it was her."

Miranda frowned. "I thought you were a kindergarten teacher."

"I am, but I work a second job to help pay for my mother's medical expenses. She's getting older and has a heart condition. I work in the evenings."

Miranda felt a shiver go down her back. "What's the name of the restaurant where you work?"

"The Sapphire Grille. It's on Wacker Drive downtown. It's near the Lyric Opera. Sometimes I play in the orchestra when someone is ill, so it's convenient."

The same restaurant they were at a few hours ago. Prescott's favorite spot. Where he used to take his lovers, according to Ivy Flores. "So you saw Quinton Preston with this woman there?"

"Yes. They'd come in for dinner once or twice a week. I waited on them a few times, but neither of them recognized me."

"And you saw this woman with Prescott at the reunion."

"Yes. I don't remember her name."

"Can you describe her?"

"Tall, dark hair. Very good looking. She had on a red dress."

"Stella La Stella?"

"Yes, that's her. She was one of the reunion committee members, wasn't she? I must have seen her name on the email invitation."

Trying to keep her composure, Miranda drew in a slow breath. "And you're certain this was the same woman who was talking to Mr. Prescott on the terrace the evening of the reunion?"

"Positive. She's stunning. It's hard not to remember her."

That was certainly true. "Did you happen to hear what they were saying to each other?"

"Yes. That's what I wanted to tell you."

A tingle of excitement nestled in Miranda's stomach. Could they finally get something solid on Stella? "Go on."

"First of all, Quinton was pretty drunk. He was leaning over the banister and swaying like he was on a rocking ship or something."

Miranda nodded while Templeton took out her notebook and made a notation. That matched what Dwight Donahue had told them last night.

"So the woman, what was her name? Stella?"

"Yes."

"Stella comes up to him and says something. I didn't hear that part. She touched his arm and Quinton jerked away from her and said, 'Get away from me. I told you I didn't want to see you again.' that was when I realized they were the couple from the restaurant. I didn't know Quinton was married to someone else."

"You learned that at the reunion?"

"Yes. Earlier I heard him chatting with his wife, telling her what a good job she'd done. She was the main coordinator."

Templeton shifted her weight. "What did Ms. La Stella do when Mr. Prescott pushed her away?"

"She told him he was drunk and he should get some coffee. He told her to mind her own business and that she'd better not make a scene."

"Then what happened?"

"Stella got angry. 'Why should I make a scene over you?' she said to him. And he said, 'I know you're still in love with me. Why else would you be stalking me all these weeks? You need to get help. You're a sick woman'."

Another match to what Donahue told them. "That's what Prescott said to her?"

"Well, his speech was slurred, but those were his words."

"What did Stella do next?"

"That was when the dance music stopped and they started to get ready to give away the prizes for that silly game everyone was playing. I didn't play, so I left."

"Was Ms. La Stella still with Mr. Prescott?" Templeton asked.

"Everyone started moving into the main room and gathering on the dance floor. I went out through one of the doors near the rear, but when I turned and looked back, they were both still standing there along the banister."

"And that was the last time you saw either of them?"

"No. I went to the ladies' room before going out. I was just washing my hands when Stella came rushing in. She hurried to one of the stalls and shut the door, but I saw she was crying. I heard her, too. I thought it was sad."

She looked down at the table again and waited.

After a moment, Miranda realized she was done. "Is there anything else?" she asked.

"No. That's what I came in to tell you. I hope it helps."

It sure did.

Templeton took out a card and handed it to Victoria. "Thank you for your cooperation, Ms. Winslow. If you think of anything else, please give me a call."

"I will," she said softly and rose.

CHAPTER TWENTY-NINE

Two minutes after Victoria Winslow left the station, Miranda burst into Demarco's office again with Parker and Templeton just behind her.

"We've got a lead."

Demarco jolted up. "A real one?"

"Yep. We just talked to a woman named Victoria Winslow who was at the party. She saw Prescott on the terrace with Stella just before the contest prizes were given out."

"So?"

Miranda went over what Winslow had told them.

"And?" Demarco still wasn't convinced.

"It explains this text conversation between Prescott and La Stella." She picked up the printout that she'd left on his desk and read it aloud.

Hi there, darling. I can't wait to see you tonight.

Are you taking me to our favorite place?

Where else? And then to the moon.

"Is that from one of the women Ivy Flores told you about?" Demarco hadn't been listening.

"It's from Stella. And it was sent this past November. Five months ago. All the pieces are starting to come together. The timeline at the party is right now, too.

"What do you mean?"

Miranda drew in a breath and tried not to sound irritated as she explained. "Stella La Stella was the one who first found Prescott hanging over the banister Saturday night. He was supposed to come in from the terrace to present the winner of the Most Likely To contest with the prize."

Demarco looked confused. "And?"

"And when Prescott didn't show, Jane sent Stella out to get him. She came back into the banquet hall only a few seconds later, yelling for help. There wouldn't be enough time for her to tie Prescott's tie to the banister and push him over, or for him to expire before Parker and the football players got to him."

"Okay." Demarco was starting to get it.

"But now we have a witness who saw Stella and Prescott together at the banister right before the prizes were given out. She says they were the last two on the terrace. And Stella was late getting to the podium. Plus when she got there, her nose was red. She'd been crying because of the things Prescott had said to her. The things that made her push him over the banister."

Demarco sat back and reached for another toothpick. "Did anyone else at the reunion party mention seeing La Stella with Prescott?"

Miranda turned to Templeton.

She seemed flustered. "We'll have to go over the interview notes again, but I don't recall anyone saying anything like that."

Miranda started to grind her teeth.

She and Parker had been on the terrace during that time. She'd seen Prescott, but he'd been way at the other end with his back to them. She'd been lost in her conversation with her mesmerizing husband, and she hadn't paid the former class president any attention.

Beside her, Templeton straightened her shoulders. "I think we have enough to bring Ms. La Stella in for questioning, sir."

Miranda nodded. "Good idea."

Parker was looking at his phone. "I believe Ms. La Stella is getting ready for the nine o'clock news right now."

Miranda glanced over his shoulder and saw the time. Almost eight-thirty. He was right.

Demarco pointed at them one by one. "Well then, you three will have to go down to the TV station and have a little chat with her, won't you?"

Miranda was speechless. Had Demarco just okayed questioning Stella?

Demarco stuck his toothpick in his mouth, got to his feet, and started tossing empty coffee cups in the trash. "I need some more of this battery acid." He scowled at the detective. "Why are you still here, Templeton? Get going. We need to close this case."

He had okayed it.

"Yes, sir," Templeton grinned.

And they all hurried out of the office before the sergeant changed his mind.

CHAPTER THIRTY

As they headed toward the cubes to get their coats, Templeton paused a moment.

"What is it, Detective?" Parker asked.

They needed to get going. Surely Templeton wasn't having second thoughts about Stella's being their prime suspect.

Looking as if she'd made an important decision, Templeton crooked a finger at them. "Come with me a minute."

"Okay, but where are we going?"

"It'll only take a minute."

Templeton led them into a hall with waist-high paneling. They went through a door at the end of it, down a flight of metal stairs, and into another hallway painted in a bland eggshell color. At a wide gray door, she swiped the badge on her lanyard, and turned on the lights as they stepped inside a huge room.

With Parker at her side, Miranda followed Templeton through rows and rows of metal lockers until they reached a large dark storage unit at the far end of the space.

Templeton took a key from her pocket, opened the unit, and Miranda found herself staring at racks of dozens of rifles and pistols.

Templeton gestured to the artillery. "Our standard issues are Glock 19s with a seventeen-round magazine. What do you think?"

Miranda hesitated. "We're going to pack to talk to the weather girl?"

The detective raised a shoulder. "You never know. I don't expect you'll need them, but I want to cover my bases. I don't want to take chances."

Or do something she'd get reprimanded for by Demarco.

Miranda turned to Parker. His expression was unreadable, but she knew what he must be thinking.

This case was never supposed to be life-threatening. That was what they had retired to get away from. And she knew he was worried about her. He always worried about her. The same way she always worried about him.

Seventeen-round Glocks were overkill. They wouldn't need them. Still, if it set Templeton's mind at ease, why not take them? And Parker wasn't saying no.

Miranda gazed over the neat rows of pistols, picked one out, and ran her hand over its smooth black finish.

Something stirred inside her.

She smiled at Templeton. "You've got shoulder holsters, too, don't you?"

CHAPTER THIRTY-ONE

Dressed in her red stretch pencil sheath with the black leather trim, Stella stood in front of the green screen in the weather spot, going over the cues on the monitor off to the side.

Partly cloudy...a warm front coming in across the western plains...humph. The real meteorologist had gotten that wrong yesterday, so everyone she knew had reminded her all day long, blaming her as if it had been her forecast. Once she was a real meteorologist, she'd get things right.

She just had to get through this little rough patch, and everything would be okay. A few more days and things would settle down.

Nerves roused in her stomach. Oh, it wasn't just a rough patch. And who knew how long it would take for things to settle down? Maybe they never would. She wanted to rub her forehead but she'd smear her makeup.

It was hard to concentrate after that visit from the police detective at Jane's yesterday. The cops wouldn't stop until they had an answer. And now that Miranda Steele and her hunky husband were involved, they were more likely than ever to find out things that were nobody's business.

She had to do something.

Think of some way to protect herself. But her head had been in a whirl ever since Saturday night. She felt like a walking zombie. She couldn't think straight.

They had made so many mistakes. Made so many bad decisions.

Her attention went to the brightly lit area with the cityscape backdrop across the floor. The anchors at the desk were finishing up and about to introduce her.

Head up, deep breath, smile.

Then from the corner of her eye, she saw movement in front of the dark padded panels across from the set, where people sometimes watched the news people at work. It was that police detective and Miranda Steele with her husband.

Stella's heart nearly stopped. How did they get in here? And what did they want?

CHAPTER THIRTY-TWO

With Templeton at the helm, they didn't need to use Parker's persuasion skills to get into the studio. Not even with Glocks under their coats.

Someone pointed them in the general direction, and with Parker and Templeton on either side of her, Miranda made her way up to the ninth floor and across a huge space with dozens of desks and chairs and computers, where news was created every day.

Now they stood before a gray padded panel under a high black ceiling tangled with scaffolding and stage lights.

The set before them wasn't exactly a hive of activity. On one side a man in a suit and a woman in a blue dress sat like statues waiting for their turn to jabber about current events. On the other side, a man in another suit was going through papers in front of a blue set. The sports guy.

And in the middle was Stella La Stella in all her glory. Her turn to be on camera.

She stood before a green screen, gesturing at it as if the map was there. Instead, she was taking her cues from a small video monitor off to the side.

Her movements were smooth, her words interesting, her smile perfect. She seemed to have a real rapport with the viewers. But underneath, Miranda could tell she was rattled.

She must have seen them.

At last, she came to the end of her spiel. "We'll be back at ten with development on that front. Will there be snow?"

The camera light blinked off and she relaxed. As the anchors began reading from their monitors again, Stella unplugged a wire attached to her ear. Then she turned, gave Miranda a glare, and started straight for her.

"What are you doing here?" she hissed in a whisper when she reached her. "How did you get in?"

"We're with the police." Miranda gestured toward Templeton.

"We need to speak with you, Ms. La Stella," the detective told her without emotion.

Stella's blue eyes flashed. "I'm working." Then she blinked as if she realized that was the wrong attitude. "Did you figure out what happened to Quinton? Have you spoken to Jane?"

Parker leaned in and spoke with a low tone that said it was no use to fight them. "Is there somewhere we can speak privately, Stella?"

Stella's lashes fluttered as she stared at him. She glanced back at the set, then gave in. "I have a desk. It's over here."

She led them out of the gray padded area and through a set of white panels forming a hall with fluorescent lights mounted at the top every few feet.

Miranda blinked at the contrast in lighting until they stepped into another open area, and the high black ceiling reappeared with its scaffolding. Here was a sea of long open desks and empty chairs. Computer screens were everywhere. On the desks, mounted in rows on a distant wall, in the windowed offices along the perimeter.

Another news making hive.

They made a few turns and ended up in an area with partitions that looked more like an office.

Stella cut through an aisle, made two more turns, and then entered one of the cubicles.

There was a narrow light gray desk with three small drawers on one side and two file-sized drawers on the other. Atop the surface was a laptop, several mirrors, a bottle of foundation, and a large hairbrush.

Stella waved at the space. "This is it. My home away from home. I only have one chair."

"Why don't you take it?" Parker said as if he were inviting her to a state dinner.

With a shrug, she plopped down into it. "What do you have to tell me?"

"We have a few questions for you, Ms. La Stella," Templeton said.

She surveyed each of them carefully. "Okay, shoot."

Miranda folded her arms. "Why don't you start by telling us about what you did at the party Saturday night."

"The party? I already told that to the police."

She'd been interviewed along with everyone else Saturday night.

"Go over it again. Just the part at the end."

Stella glared at Miranda. "You were there."

"Humor us."

Stella let out a huff. "At the end?"

"You know what I mean." When she found Prescott.

She shrugged. "I was standing at the podium with Jane as she gave out the prizes for the Most Likely To contest. She got to the first prize winner. It was Miranda here. Quinton was supposed to come out from the terrace and give it to her. That was my idea. You know, the winner of the Most Likely To contest getting the prize from the Most Likely to Succeed? Anyway, he didn't appear, so Jane asked me to go out and get him. And when I did—" She put both hands over her mouth with an anguished gasp. "That's when I found him." She reached for a tissue from a container on the desk. "I don't know if I can go through this again."

Miranda didn't feel much sympathy. "You don't have to. We're interested in what happened before that."

"Before?"

"When Jane first went to the podium and started speaking, you weren't there. You didn't get there until she finished talking about the rest of the committee."

Stella looked genuinely confused. Or was she coming up with a story? "Oh, now I remember. I went to the ladies' room."

"Before that."

She frowned. "I don't know what you mean, Miranda."

Templeton cleared her throat. "We have a witness who saw you talking with Mr. Prescott just before the prizes were given out, Ms. La Stella."

Stella's face turned pale. "What?"

"She heard you arguing with him," Miranda said. "He told you to stop stalking him."

Stella blinked as if Miranda had just slapped her. Then she let out a laugh. "That's a bald-faced lie, and you know it. I don't stalk men. I have to keep them from stalking me." She looked at her phone. "I have another segment to do."

She got up and started to go, but Templeton blocked her way. "We'll need you to come down to the station with us when you're finished."

Her jaw went slack. Then she pulled herself together. "Of course. I always cooperate with the police."

"Do you mind if we look around here while you finish up?" Miranda asked as Templeton stepped back.

"Do whatever you want."

And the weather girl hurried away, no doubt trying to find her composure before she had to go on camera again.

CHAPTER THIRTY-THREE

Miranda stood on tiptoe and peeked over the cube wall to make sure Stella was gone. When she was sure about that, she started for the desk.

Templeton shook her head. "Do you really think she would leave evidence here?"

"It's worth looking. She gave us permission. That makes it legal, doesn't it?" Miranda pulled out a drawer and breathed in a perfumey scent. The compartment wasn't very big, but it seemed to hold a department store of makeup. Powders, eyeshadow palettes, brushes and pencils and eye liners, about a dozen lipsticks in fifty shades of red.

Templeton turned to Parker. "What do you think?"

"She did exhibit the signs of guilt." Parker opened one of the file size drawers on the other side of the desk. "This is empty."

Miranda reached for the second drawer on her side. In this one she found hair brushes, a curling iron, and scrunchies.

Parker opened the bottom drawer of the cabinet and again found it empty.

Templeton was getting antsy. "Just put everything back the way you found it. I don't want her filing a complaint."

"I think we're the only ones who'll be filing something tonight." As in charges.

But Miranda took the time to do what Templeton said. Then she opened the last drawer on her side. The largest one. Scarves and necklaces. One by one, she pulled them out. Long gold chains, deep red beads, a string of seashells. Infinity scarves in assorted colors, kerchiefs, earbobs.

"Be careful not to snag anything."

"It's a wonder she didn't do that herself. Wait a second." Miranda stopped with her arm raised, a lacy red thing dangling from it. Her breath caught as she stared down at the bottom of the drawer. "Is that what I think it is?"

Parker and Templeton came over to see what she was talking about.

"Don't move." Templeton took out her cell.

Bending over, she snapped several shots of the inside of the drawer, then pulled a blue plastic glove out of her pocket. She slipped it on and reached inside the drawer. Carefully, she removed what Miranda had spotted.

Miranda's heartbeat kicked up as she gazed at it in disbelief. A four-by-six glossy that had to have been taken years ago.

Stella La Stella and Quinton Prescott arm in arm, standing under an arch of flowers. Stella in a sparkling blue gown holding a bouquet of red roses, Quinton in a matching tux. Crowns on their heads and sashes across their torsos.

The prom king and queen.

"Well, now," Templeton said. "Why would someone hold onto that all these years?"

Miranda could make a good guess. "Let's go find out."

They hurried back through the cubes, the newsroom, and the makeshift hall. By the time they reached the gray padded viewing area, Miranda's blood was pounding.

And then she came to a halt as she caught sight of the set.

The weather station was dark.

The anchors were finished reporting, too, and the female anchor was removing her earpiece.

Miranda hurried over to her. "Where's Ms. La Stella?"

She frowned.

"The weather lady." Miranda pointed to the dark set.

"Oh. She finished her session and left."

Must have been short. "Where did she go?"

"Home, I suppose."

Miranda felt like she'd been punched in the chest. That couldn't be right. "She didn't have a coat or purse with her."

The woman gestured toward a dark area off to the side hung with a black curtain. "We have lockers back there. I saw her heading there a little while ago."

"Do you know if she took the train to work?"

"Not at this hour. Since she got this spot, she's been driving in. She likes to brag about that gold Impala of hers."

Sounded like Stella. "Thanks."

Her head spinning, Miranda returned to the viewing area in time to see Parker use Templeton's glove to slip the photo into his front coat pocket.

A lot of good it did them now. "She's in the wind," she told them.

Templeton looked stunned. "What do you mean?"

"She left the building."

Templeton scratched her head to hide her agitation. "She probably went to her residence."

"A fair assumption," Parker said.

"That's what the anchor said." Miranda felt like punching something. "She's there probably destroying evidence right now." No, she couldn't have gotten there yet. Could she?

Parker started toward the exit. "Let's see if we can get there in time to stop her."

CHAPTER THIRTY-FOUR

In the Jaguar, with its five-hundred and fifty hp turbocharged engine, Parker zoomed through the night down West Addison, past old brick apartment and office buildings, and through the neighborhoods. Templeton was behind them for a while, blue lights flashing, but soon they left her in the dust.

Good thing she had texted them the address.

According to the text, Stella lived in a house in Oak Park on Harvey Avenue, down the street from the Presbyterian church.

Parker turned onto Harlem and roared through the quiet darkened streets, reaching their destination in another seven minutes, and beating Templeton there.

As he pulled up to the curb, Miranda stared out at the pale gray stucco home with a porch and white trim. An outside light was on, but the windows were dark.

"That's funny."

"What is?"

"I could swear this is the house Stella grew up in." Miranda thought she might have been to a party here once.

"It is."

She spun around. "How do you know that?"

Parker gave her his signature wry grin. "I did some background research on her yesterday."

"Oh, you did, did you?"

"I did. Her parents passed away when Stella was ten. Her grandmother raised her in this house until her first marriage. Stella inherited the place after her death."

A sad story. "I don't see her car."

There were several others parked along the street, probably belonging to the neighbors, but no gaudy gold Impala with a LA STELLA tag.

"There's a garage in the back."

"Yeah."

Typical of the near suburbs, the houses were bunched together with just enough space to walk between them. Garages were detached from the homes and accessed through an alley in the back.

While Miranda peered at the windows of the house, trying to detect movement, Templeton's Tahoe finally pulled up behind them. She'd turned off her police lights.

Miranda got out of the Jag and jogged over as Templeton climbed out of her front seat.

"We think her car is in the garage in back, but there's no sign of life," she told her.

Templeton nodded.

"So what's the plan?"

Templeton studied the house with a bland expression. "Why don't we go knock on the door?"

Sounded good to her.

Miranda turned and led the way down the walkway, then up the steps to the front door. She let Templeton ring the bell.

It was an old fashioned ding-dong.

No dog barked. No footsteps sounded.

The detective waited a moment, then rang again.

Silence.

Templeton gave Miranda and Parker a look of disgust and raised her hand to knock.

Still nothing.

This time, Templeton turned into a cop. She banged hard on the door. "Chicago police. We need to speak with you, Ms. La Stella."

Still no sound from inside.

Gritting her teeth, Miranda turned around to scan the street. Everything looked dark and quiet. Except for a skinny man in a plaid jacket and old jeans coming across the yard toward them. Under the porch light, he looked around fifty, and his gray hair was long and tied back in a ponytail. He was carrying a canvas bag in his hand.

"Are you looking for Ms. La Stella?" he called out.

Templeton came down the steps and handed the man her card. "Detective Shirley Templeton of the Chicago PD. Yes, we are. Do you know her?"

He took the card and eyed it with a raised brow. "I've known her since she was a little girl. She's a firecracker, that one."

"And you are?"

"Harvey Scalzo. I've lived across the street all my life." He pointed to the house behind him.

Miranda hurried over to the neighbor. "Mr. Scalzo, do you know where Ms. La Stella is right now? We believe she came home after work tonight, but she's not answering the door."

Scalzo eyed her, then narrowed an eye at Parker, who was now beside her. "And you are?"

Parker extended a hand. "Wade Parker of the Parker Investigative Agency. This is my partner, Miranda Steele. We're assisting the police in an investigation."

Reluctantly, Scalzo put Templeton's card in his pocket and shook hands.

"We'd appreciate your cooperation in this matter, Mr. Scalzo," Templeton said with just a hint of warning in her tone.

Scalzo looked like he couldn't imagine what this was about. But slowly he nodded. "Stella did come home tonight, but she took off right away. It was maybe fifteen minutes before you pulled up in that spiffy Jag." He turned to admire the vehicle.

Miranda wanted to spit. She knew that sneaky bitch would run.

Scalzo raised his arm. "She asked me to hold this bag for her."

It was a leopard print leather tote bag with a zipper along the top.

"We'd like to take a look at that," said Templeton.

"I don't want to get her into any trouble."

Templeton turned pure cop. "Mr. Scalzo, Ms. La Stella is wanted for questioning in a homicide."

"Homicide?" He took a rickety step back as if he might fall over. "Stella wouldn't be involved in anything like that. She's a good kid."

So good, she's running from the police. Miranda had a thought. "You wouldn't have happened to have seen any men with Ms. La Stella over here, would you?" She jabbed her thumb back at the house.

"Men?"

"One in particular. Tall guy, muscular, curly blond hair?" Scalzo either hadn't seen the news story about Prescott or hadn't made the connection.

"No. Stella didn't have men over. Like I said, she was a good kid."

Templeton ignored the comment. "May we look at the bag?"

"I guess so, but I'm sure you won't find anything."

He handed it over, and Templeton unzipped it. While Parker held the bag open by its straps, and Templeton snapped photos with her phone, Miranda pulled out the contents.

More scarves, some towels, underwear, including a black negligee, and at the very bottom, an amber plastic bottle with a pharmacy label.

Using a scarf in lieu of a plastic glove, Miranda held the bottle up to read it and sucked in a breath.

It was Prescott's prescription for oxycodone.

"The missing refill," Parker said grimly as he read the date on the label.

It was only about two-thirds full, just like the first bottle.

Templeton took the bottle from Miranda and gently put it back into the bag. "I'll have to take this with us, Mr. Scalzo."

The poor man looked lost. He hadn't done a very good job of keeping the bag for his neighbor. "I'm sure Ms. La Stella didn't do anything wrong. Is there anything I can do to help her?"

"Not right now," Templeton said. "Thank you for your cooperation."

Looking guilty and bewildered, the neighbor plodded back across the street while they moved back to Templeton's Tahoe.

"I need to call this in and put out a BOLO on our weather girl." Templeton put Stella's tote bag in the backseat and dialed her phone.

Miranda kicked at the asphalt while she listened to Templeton give the order. She glanced at Parker. His expression was grim, but she could tell he was thinking about something.

After a moment Templeton hung up and stuck her phone back in her pocket. Her face was as gloomy as Parker's.

"What is it?" Miranda said.

"Kadera said the prints on Prescott's tie came back from the lab."

Miranda took a step closer to the car. "And?"

"There were only two sets. Prescott's and La Stella's."

"She did it. She killed him." Miranda had been right all along, but there was no joy in that knowledge.

Instead she felt a heavy emptiness. And more sorrow for Jane. Stella was supposed to be her friend.

"I've sent a squad car over to the Prescott home," Templeton said. "I figure that's where La Stella would go. Heading there now to pick her up. You don't have to come unless you want to."

Before Miranda could open her mouth to reply, Parker put a hand on her arm. "If it's all the same to you, Detective, we'll sit this one out."

He was done with this case, and Miranda couldn't blame him. The police had their killer. No need to stick around for the aftermath.

"Sure." Templeton nodded. "I'll update you in the morning."

"We'll look forward to your call."

CHAPTER THIRTY-FIVE

Back in the Jag, Miranda waited until Templeton's Tahoe had turned left onto Division at the stop sign, and Parker had crossed the street and continued north.

Then she couldn't help but ask the obvious question. "You didn't want to help bring Stella in?"

She expected him to remind her they were supposed to be retired.

Instead, he said, "I have another idea."

"Oh?" Parker always did have a sneaky side.

He drove north to the next stop sign, turned west, and continued down a side street where lights twinkled warmly in the closely spaced homes. "As I said before, after I contacted Prescott's doctor yesterday afternoon, I did a little digging into Ms. La Stella's background."

And hadn't told her everything.

Miranda twisted in her seat to face him. "And what did you learn?"

"About a sad and sordid tale."

She had already guessed the sad part from what he'd said about Stella's grandmother. "Spill."

Parker turned right at a fancy brick home with a turret. "First, after high school, Stella earned a degree in Communications from the University of Illinois. After graduating from college, she moved to New York and attended a modeling school."

"She wanted to be a fashion model?" But it made sense. Stella had always sought the limelight.

"Apparently. She had little success and was often rejected for being too 'curvy'."

"Hmm." And to think, back in the day Miranda had been a little jealous of Stella's curves.

"However, she managed to get an agent and married him two years after she moved to New York."

Wow. Miranda thought of the list of ex-husbands Stella had rattled off at the reunion. "Which one was that? Williams?"

"Douglas Williams, who went by the name Bobo. Three years later, she divorced him for adultery. He was sleeping with three of his models."

"Ouch. Wait. How exactly did you learn all this?"

Parker turned left onto North Avenue and they drove past the lights of restaurants and long brick office buildings. "Stella used to post personal information on social media, though she hasn't recently, and I couldn't find anything about Prescott. I checked out her claims about her ex-husbands in the various records databases, and what she'd said was basically true."

And Parker had kept it all to himself. "Okay. Go on."

"It seems Stella was awarded a hefty alimony in her divorce from Williams. She used it to move to Los Angeles and start a movie career."

From modeling to the movies. "I have a feeling that didn't work out as planned."

"Actually, she appeared in a few commercials. Then she caught the eye of a director named Abbott Conan Perry."

"Her second husband."

Parker nodded. "For about two years. Then Stella found him naked in their swimming pool with one of his starlets. He claimed to be developing her career. Stella jumped into the pool fully clothed and tried to strangle Perry."

Miranda's brows rose. "Now that's interesting."

"Yes. After the divorce was settled, and Stella was awarded another sizable alimony, she moved back to Chicago and eventually married her third husband."

Miranda recalled the name. "Schimmelpfennig."

"Dr. Heinrich Schimmelpfennig, a Mathematics professor at a local community college."

That was a switch. "She wanted someone stable after two failed marriages, I'd guess."

"Perhaps. However, three years after they said 'I do,' Schimmelpfennig was arrested and convicted for possession and distribution of child pornography."

"Another creep? Stella was batting a thousand, wasn't she?" Miranda was starting to feel sorry for her.

"Unfortunately."

They were on River Road now. She peered over the concrete barrier into the dark ravine where the muddy Des Plaines River ran. "So after all that, when Prescott rejected her—like he did all the women he slept with—she snapped. Instead of jumping into a Hollywood pool and strangling him, she hangs him over a banister twenty stories over Michigan Avenue."

"Possibly."

"Okay, then what does Stella's history with her exes have to do with why we're not at Jane's picking her up?"

"I don't think Stella would have gone to Jane's."

She leaned back in her seat and stared at the taillights stretching out before them in the darkness. "You're right. She'd know that's the first place the cops would look for her. But where did she go? And where are we going?"

They definitely weren't heading back to the hotel.

"The most pertinent detail I learned about Stella yesterday is that she has an aunt in Kenosha, Wisconsin."

Miranda sat up again. "Wisconsin?"

"Stella stayed with her about six months after her divorce from Schimmelpfennig. Until her grandmother passed away and left her the house in Oak Park. That was when she got the job at the news station."

Miranda pondered that revelation as Parker continued on through the suburbs until he reached the entrance ramp to I-294 in Schiller Park.

"So that's where we're headed? To Wisconsin?"

"It's over an hour's drive, but worth the time to check out, wouldn't you agree?"

"Of course, I agree. But why didn't you tell Templeton about the aunt?"

"For one thing, she'd send a legion of police to the aunt's."

"And spook Stella enough to run again." If she was there.

"And the idea is just a hunch. If it's wrong and we were to send the police on a wild goose chase—"

"Templeton would look bad in front of Demarco."

"Precisely."

Miranda thought about the way Demarco had scolded her over the news reporters. "He's hard on her. You picked up on that too?"

"I did. Demarco seems to be the type who likes to handle things himself. It takes him a while to trust his employees. If we find Stella at her aunt's, we can contact Templeton and she can alert the local authorities to apprehend her."

"And Templeton will look like the hero."

"Yes."

She loved his generous side. "And if we need to, we can detain Stella." She patted the shoulder holster under her coat.

Parker scowled at that idea. "Let's hope that won't be necessary."

He'd had enough shootouts for a lifetime, and so had she. Especially the last one.

She shook off the grim thought. "Okay. How long a head start does Stella have? Thirty minutes?"

"Given the time we spent talking to her neighbor, I'd say so."

She looked at the time on the dash. Almost midnight. It would be after one when they got to the aunt's house. She was up for it.

Settling back for the long ride, Miranda grinned.

They might catch Stella just as she was climbing into bed.

CHAPTER THIRTY-SIX

The monotonous highway and steady glow of taillights on the interstate must have put her to sleep.

Miranda woke to the sensation of the car slowing down. Raising her head she squinted. "Are we at the aunt's house?"

Parker's low steady voice caressed her ears. "We're at a toll booth near Waukegan. We have about twenty miles to go."

She sat up and stretched. A long line of vehicles were at a standstill in front of them. "What's taking so long?"

"Only one booth is open."

"Great." She groaned out loud. "We're going to miss her."

"Not if she's spending the night at her aunt's."

Good point. Stella would have to stay at the aunt's house at least a few hours before taking off. Unless she thought the police would figure out she was there.

Frustrated, Miranda rolled down the window and leaned out.

Alongside the road was nothing but grass and the outline of trees disappearing into the darkness. The cool night air whispered against her face as she tried to count how many cars were in front of them.

A big black SUV. A gray compact. A little green Honda. She could smell their fumes. The line rolled forward, and she caught the gleam of a gold bumper.

"Wait a minute." She wriggled onto her knees on the soft leather.

"What is it?"

She pushed herself halfway out of the window and squinted.

Then she grinned. "Yep. There's a gold Impala four cars ahead of us. Last three letters of the tag are 'L-L-A'. It's her."

"Something must have slowed her down."

Miranda sat back down and rolled up the window. "You were going at a pretty good clip before I fell asleep. Maybe she had to stop for gas and got a bite to eat."

"Possibly."

"Likely." Feeling cocky, she gave him a light punch on the arm with her fist. He returned a playful scowl.

There were more cars in front of Stella's. Miranda counted the stops and starts as they moved through the tollbooth one by one. Finally, the eighteen wheeler in front of the Impala rolled up, screeching and belching to a stop.

After what seemed like an eternity, with another blast of noise and smoke, it moved on into the night.

Now it was Stella's turn.

Didn't take her long. She must have had exact change.

As the Impala zoomed away, Miranda looked down at the cup holder and saw rolls of quarters, dimes, and nickels. "You've been thinking about this a while."

"It never hurts to be prepared."

He must have gotten the change at the hotel.

The green Honda was at the booth now. Miranda's stomach tensed as the Impala's taillights disappeared into the night.

"We'll catch up to her," Parker said, picking up on her anxiety.

They had to.

While the gray compact took its turn, Miranda grabbed a roll of coins and began opening them. She watched the taillights of the black SUV go through the booth as she counted out the change.

At last it was their turn.

"Good evening," Parker handed the coins to the mustached teller in a ball cap and glasses who appeared to be in his late forties.

"Good evening, sir," he said in a thick Chicago accent. "I apologize for the delay. Technical difficulties."

"Our modern world."

"Exactly," the man grinned.

"Did you happen to notice who was driving the gold Impala that came through a few vehicles ago?"

The teller seemed surprised by the question. "The brunette? Did I ever. Man, she was a looker. Why? Do you know her?"

"Our neighbor."

Parker was smooth.

"Well, well. Small world isn't it? Maybe you'll catch up to her."

"Perhaps we will."

"Have a safe trip." The man raised the gate, and Parker zoomed through.

CHAPTER THIRTY-SEVEN

Past the tollbooth, the night sky was a sheet of dull charcoal with only the tall turnpike lamps illuminating the eight lanes of traffic below.

Miranda peered through the windshield. The air was growing misty, blurring the taillights and making it hard to distinguish the vehicles.

More of that light rain.

Parker sped up to get around the semi on the right, the Jag roaring against the grinding truck engine.

As they passed the truck, she spotted the black SUV, but other cars were scattered across the lanes, some of which had just joined the pack from an on-ramp from the plaza on the left where a row of orange traffic barrels marked the lanes.

She didn't see the gold Impala anywhere.

"Have we lost her?"

Parker turned on the wipers and the defrost. "We'll find her again. There isn't an exit for another two miles. We should be able to catch her before then."

She hoped so.

Miranda rolled down the window and rolled it up again to clear the condensation. She strained to see the vehicles going around the curve up ahead. There was a wooden fence alongside the highway. Beyond it, bare tree branches stretched into the night.

Nowhere to go except straight ahead.

Suddenly a glint off a gold bumper flickered through the cloud of metal and lights.

Miranda shot up in her seat. "There she is."

"I see her." Parker sped up, crossed two lanes, and eased into Stella's lane just behind a blue Audi.

"Do you think she saw us?" Miranda was wishing they were in Parker's neutral Mazda instead of a flashy red Jaguar.

"Let's assume she didn't."

Best they could do.

They drove on. After a little while, they passed the exit Parker had mentioned.

Stella held her lane. So did the Audi.

"So now what? Do we follow her all the way to her aunt's house?"

Parker's hands were steady on the wheel as he peered through the windshield. "Assuming she's going there."

Isn't that what they'd been assuming since they left Stella's house? But what if they were wrong? What if she was heading farther north? Maybe to Canada? They couldn't take her down themselves. "Are you saying we should contact Templeton?"

"It would be protocol."

"But we should make absolutely sure it's Stella first."

"That would be wise." Parker slowed as he followed the curve of the road.

The Impala sped up. Beyond the Audi, Miranda could see most of the plate now. "L-A space S-T-E-L. It's definitely her."

"Go ahead and call Templeton."

"On it."

She dialed Templeton's number, told her they'd found Stella, and gave her their location. "That's right. Just past 173 on I-94 near Waukegan. We think she's headed for her aunt's house in Kenosha."

Since Templeton had been riding around the neighborhoods for over an hour hunting the suspect with no luck, she was delighted to hear the news. She said she'd contact the local authorities right away.

But just as Miranda hung up, the blue Audi switched lanes and headed for an exit ramp.

They were out in the open.

"She hasn't necessarily seen us," Parker said, reading Miranda's thoughts.

True. Stella showed no sign of that. They just had to be patient. Just had to hold on.

Parker slowed, and Miranda hoped someone would get in front of him for cover, but nobody did.

That was when Stella sped up.

"She's made us."

"Apparently so." There was firm determination in Parker's voice. He wasn't going to let her get away.

They glided under the overpass. Another semi got between them and the Impala.

"She won't see us now," Parker said with a flash of anger.

He switched lanes and pulled past the semi and another sedan that had come out of nowhere.

The Impala was way ahead of them now. Again he sped up.

Miranda held her breath.

Then she turned her head and spotted a squad car coming down the entrance ramp on the right. "Uh oh."

"It appears the police here are quick responders."

Templeton was a fast worker, too. "His lights aren't flashing. Maybe Templeton told him to approach with caution."

The police car zoomed into the lane, half a car length behind Stella.

Stella floored it.

"She definitely knows we're after her now."

The distance between Stella and the squad car lengthened. Stella pulled across two lanes. The horns of the cars she'd cut off wailed in protest, but she'd escaped the cop. For the moment.

Parker studied the situation.

Then he zoomed forward and switched lanes again. Before Miranda could take a breath, he'd pulled up right behind Stella, regaining the squad car's last position.

The cop was in the next lane on Miranda's side. He turned on his lights.

Ignoring the warning, once again Stella soared ahead.

Miranda had had enough of this. "Can you get beside her?"

"With pleasure." Parker hit the accelerator hard.

They soared forward and reached the Impala's rear in a matter of seconds. As she eyed the vanity plate, Miranda heard the cop coming up behind them.

Parker switched lanes again and zoomed up next to Stella's car. They had to be going over ninety.

As the Jag's hood reached the Impala's, Miranda peeked inside the vehicle. She could see panic on Stella's face as she steered.

Quickly Miranda rolled down the window. "Pull over," she yelled, spitting out the hair flying over her face.

Eyes glaring, Stella rolled down her window, too. "Leave me alone, Miranda."

"Pull over," Miranda screamed again. "The cops are onto you."

"All because of you. You're the same no-account bitch you were in high school." She raised her hand.

Miranda looked down and saw Stella was holding a black snub-nose revolver.

"Look out!"

Without warning, Stella fired.

A flashback of Boston went through Miranda's head.

Parker hit the brake. The Jaguar squealed and fishtailed. The bullet skidded across the pavement and into the night.

Thank God, she hadn't hit anyone.

Not wanting to be involved in the antics, other vehicles began to pull over to the side.

Now Miranda was really mad.

Recalling the Glock Templeton had issued her, she reached under her coat for her shoulder holster and pulled it out.

They were half a car length behind the Impala now, still in the next lane.

Leaning out the window, she took aim at the rear left tire and fired.

Stella veered, and the shot missed.

The cop's siren was screaming now. And he'd been joined by several other squad cars. Miranda had no idea where they'd come from.

But the Jag was still in the best position.

"Get closer," she yelled to Parker.

"I have a better idea. Get inside and hold on tight."

She did, and held her breath as he roared ahead and jammed the Jag's hood right into that vanity tag.

The crunch of metal made Miranda's blood run cold. But she had to smile at the nice dent Parker had made in Stella's bumper.

Still, the bitch wasn't fazed. She sped up again.

"She isn't stopping."

"No."

Glancing at the signs, Miranda saw they weren't too far from the state line.

Not good.

Parker wasn't finished. He pulled out of the lane, zoomed around to Stella's side again. This time, he didn't pull up even with her, and he didn't wait for Miranda to shout at the woman.

He eased the car over and rammed into her side.

The vibration and screech of metal made Miranda's teeth chatter. "That ought to do it."

But it didn't. Stella just kept going.

Amazing what desperation could make you do.

The repetitious whine of the police sirens were getting on Miranda's nerves. She felt as if she were caught up in some surreal dream where she'd forever be chasing the former prom queen.

But then a squad car whizzed around them, pulled right in front of the Impala and slowed to block her.

Stella swerved and tried to get into the right lane.

Another squad came up beside her.

She was trapped.

She started to slow. As the second squad decelerated to let her pull over, she swerved around the police cars, and sped away again.

"That bitch!" Miranda screamed. "Get me close to her again."

Without a word, Parker put the Jag to the test. He flew past the police cars and managed to pull up to the rear of the Impala once again.

He switched lanes. "Go for it."

Miranda rolled down the window, steadied her Glock, and fired.

This time she didn't miss. She hit the rear tire right in the rubber.

The tire exploded into pieces, and the Impala went spinning off to the shoulder, coming to a stop on an embankment, facing the opposite direction.

The squad cars pulled over to surround the car, but before the officers could open their doors, Stella scrambled out of her Impala and headed off through the wet grass alongside the road.

Parker brought the Jag to a halt with a screech.

Miranda jumped out, gun drawn. "Where's she going?"

"She doesn't have many options."

Beyond the grass there was nothing but thick brush and forest. Stella was along the edge of it, hobbling along in her high heels.

Miranda was glad for her pumps as she raced after her.

The next second Parker was at her side. "Be careful, Miranda."

He was worried about what Stella might do now.

But they had to stop her. Miranda fired a shot into the weeds. "Give it up, Stella."

Stella stopped and turned around. "Why are you trying to destroy me?"

She still had the revolver in her hand.

She was starting to raise her gun when Parker appeared at her side.

How he got there so fast, Miranda would never know. He grabbed Stella's wrist, twisted the gun out of her hand, and it fell to the ground.

Then three officers were on her.

"You're under arrest, ma'am," one of them barked, as another one scooped up the gun from the grass.

They had her.

Her chest heaving and the police lights flashing all around her, Miranda watched as an officer put Stella in handcuffs and read her her rights.

CHAPTER THIRTY-EIGHT

Once again Miranda sat between Parker and Templeton in the green interrogation room at the Larrabee station.

This time with Stella La Stella across from her.

She was still in her red dress with the black leather trim that she'd worn on TV that night. Her thick black hair was tangled around her face, and her cheeks were smeared with her makeup.

The former prom queen was a mess.

"Let me ask you again, Ms. La Stella." Templeton tapped the prom photo of Stella and Quinton with her finger. "What was this doing in your desk at the television station?"

Stella sniffed and looked down tenderly at the photo. "I found this among the pictures we were going through for the reunion. I thought it would hurt Jane's feelings if she saw it, so I took it and put it in my desk at work."

Miranda didn't buy that one. She folded her arms and sat back. "Why don't you walk us through how you and Prescott really got back together."

Stella stuck out her chin and gave her a glare, but she had to talk. "It was last July. Like I told you at Jane's house. We saw each other on the train into work."

"And then what happened?"

She hunched a shoulder. "I guess I thought that old spark between us was still there. Quinton felt it, too. He asked me out to lunch."

"Where did you go?"

"A place near his law firm. It's called The Sapphire Grille."

Drawing in a breath, Miranda glanced at Parker. Just like Victoria Winslow had told them.

Stella continued. "We started to talk, you know. Catch up on things. He told me about his career as a corporate lawyer and that he had married Jane Anderson. I was surprised."

"Why?"

She rolled her eyes. "Jane Anderson. She was the most boring person I could think of. Quinton had always craved excitement."

He'd gotten a lot of excitement in the past three years, hadn't he?

"I wasn't surprised when he said his marriage wasn't going well, and he was thinking of getting a divorce. He said he'd married Jane because she gave him stability. She was the type who was never rattled. She always knew where everything went and when everything should happen. She was a rock. Like I said. Boring."

She sat back and took a sip of the coffee Templeton had given her. Wincing at it, she set the cup back down.

"Go on," Parker prompted.

"Quinton said after the kids came along, he and Jane had fallen into a routine. She took care of the house and the boys. He worked at his career. After he was promoted and had to work so many long hours, they just drifted apart. They weren't much more than roommates now. Sometimes they'd go for a whole week without saying a word to each other. He began to look elsewhere."

"You knew about his affairs?"

"Some of them. I guessed there were more. But when we got together, it was different. It was magic. I hadn't thought of him in years, but after the third dinner date, I was under his spell. I fell back in love with him."

Miranda glanced at Parker. Here we go. "And you went to bed with him."

"Not right away. We started seeing each other for dinner the nights he stayed in the city. He kept inviting me to his room. I told him no. That's the best way to lose a man. I knew I had to wait until I had him reeled in. It took months."

Miranda watched the emotion rising in Stella's piercing blue eyes. This time she didn't think it was an act.

"And then one night I said yes. Oh, not to going back to his room. Never play on his turf. I told him to get us a room in one of the best hotels in the city. I told him make it a suite. I said I'd wait for him there at nine o'clock with a surprise."

She looked down and began stroking one of her chipped fingernails.

"What happened?"

"What happened? He didn't show, the bastard."

"He stood you up?"

"Yes. I wanted to kill him. I had my little snub nose revolver with me. The one the officers took from me tonight," she added with a growl. "It's legal and I know how to use it. And that night, if I had seen Quinton, I swear I would have shot him right between the eyes. But I didn't see him. I didn't hear from him the next three weeks. Well, I decided, I guess the strategy didn't work. And then I got an email from Jane about the reunion party. She was asking for help planning it. I'll give her help, I thought."

She put her face in her hands.

"And what happened?"

Stella looked down at the photo again. This time with resentment. She lifted a shoulder. "I started working on the reunion with her and we became friends."

A bit of a jump there.

Templeton took out the oxycodone prescription and set it in the center of the table. "How did this come to be in your possession?"

Stella's eyes went wide as she looked down at the bottle. "I—I don't know what you mean."

"Your neighbor gave it to us."

Her face twisted in a flash of anger, then she turned all innocence. "Neighbor?"

"Mr. Scalzo?"

"I don't know. Maybe he killed Quinton." She glared at Templeton. "I didn't kill him. I loved him." She looked to Parker for sympathy as tears began to run down her cheeks. "I'm innocent. I swear to you, I'm innocent."

Templeton held up the oxycodone bottle. "That's not what the evidence says."

All at once, Stella pulled herself together and straightened her shoulders. "I think it's time for me to get a lawyer."

So that was it. They were done.

"Very well, Ms. La Stella. I'll have an officer escort you to your cell. You're under arrest for murder." Templeton rose and started out.

Miranda sat staring at the woman, wanting to come across the table and strangle the truth out of her.

But she had to play by the rules.

Parker touched her shoulder as an officer entered the room to take Stella away.

"Yeah," she told him. "I'm coming."

Out in the hall, Templeton shook Miranda's hand, then Parker's. "I can't thank you two enough for your help on this case. Especially with the apprehension of the suspect."

"You're welcome."

"Is that it?" Miranda said.

"That's it. The DA says we have a solid circumstantial case. The oxycodone prescription proves premeditation. More than a crime of passion when Prescott told La Stella he didn't want to leave his wife for her." Templeton straightened with an air of triumph. "It's enough for a first degree murder charge."

CHAPTER THIRTY-NINE

Miranda sat on the bed in the hotel staring blankly at the time on her phone. It was after three in the morning.

She was totally spent.

She should be elated. They had put away a killer. They had closed the case. But all she could think of was Stella La Stella in that interrogation room crying and insisting she was innocent.

As she got into bed, Parker reached for her and pulled her close, kissing her forehead. "It's over."

"It doesn't feel like it."

"I know."

She lifted her head. "You feel the same?"

"Some cases leave you with an empty feeling. You've never had one quite like this."

No, she hadn't. She didn't like it.

Parker pushed back a strand of her hair. "This might give you some closure. Yesterday when I was digging into Prescott's financials, I discovered something."

Something else he hadn't told her about? "What?"

"A life insurance policy for three million dollars."

She pushed up to stare at him as her jaw dropped. "Whoa!" Then she thought a moment. "If Stella knew about that policy or guessed there was one, that gives her a motive for befriending Jane."

"Exactly. Prescott was also hiding some funds in an offshore account."

"To keep them from Jane if she wanted a divorce?"

"Or anyone else who might try to sue him."

She shook a finger at him. "One of the women he was sleeping with."

"Most likely." Parker caught her hand and kissed the wagging finger.

She laid back down snuggled her head against his shoulder. "Well, at least Jane and the boys will be well taken care of."

"Yes. I'm glad of that."

Not just because Jane was her friend, but because of all she was going through. Miranda loved Parker's compassionate nature.

He stroked her back for awhile, then spoke again. "There's also the charge to Prescott's credit card for the hotel room."

"The one where he was supposed to meet Stella back in November?"

"Yes. The date of the charge is the day after the date on the first oxycodone prescription."

Her eyes popped open. "Prescott's broken toe. That's why he stood Stella up."

"Precisely."

"And when she went over to Jane's, she must have realized that. So did she and Prescott get back together? Were they doing the dirty all the time Stella was pretending to be Jane's friend? Or was she going after him all the time, getting rebuffed by him over and over until she decided to kill him?"

"Stalking him, as Donahue said Prescott called it." Parker didn't hide the irritation in his tone.

"Right."

"We don't know what happened between Stella and Prescott, but at some point Stella took the second oxycodone prescription out of Jane's house."

Miranda sat up again to gesture with her hands. "And Jane was too busy to notice. So Stella plots and comes up with a scheme to off her lover if he doesn't leave his wife for her. Or because he keeps rejecting her. She confronts him at the reunion in one last ditch effort, but he says no. And then what? She spikes his drink?"

"She probably did that while they were talking."

Miranda frowned. "But what if he had said yes?"

"No doubt she knew that was wishful thinking."

"Okay. So he tells her he doesn't want anything more to do with her. Angry and hungry for revenge, she ties the end of his tie to that banister and shoves him over the side, letting him hang there." She made the motions in the air. "Then she bursts into tears and runs to the ladies room."

"According to Ms. Winslow."

"She pulls herself together, goes to the podium, and pretends to find him on the terrace. That was some acting job."

"She is in the media, and she did spend time in Hollywood."

"Yeah," Miranda smirked. Then she had to frown. "I don't know. Something still isn't right."

"What do you think isn't right?" Wariness laced Parker's tone.

She thought a long moment, then she knew. "Pride."

"Pride?"

"Stella said the idea of her stalking Prescott was a bold-faced lie. She said men stalked her, not the other way around. I just can't see her as being that desperate."

Parker considered that, then pulled her back to his side. "Her lawyer may use that as her defense. The courts will sort out the details. It's out of our hands now."

She guessed it was. But it was hard to let go.

He began to kiss her face, her eyes, her lips. "I'd like to take you sightseeing tomorrow." He wanted her to forget about tonight, about this case.

She wanted to think through everything, find something more solid. Real closure. But there was nothing more to work with, and the intoxicating taste of Parker's lips was too much to resist.

She pressed in close to him. "Sightseeing, huh?"

"Sightseeing." His hands slipped under the sheets and over her skin, rousing her.

She sucked in a gasp of pleasure, let go of her thoughts, and gave in to him.

And though they were both dead tired, they made love like newlyweds, giving what remained of their energy to each other.

At last, when there was no more strength left in them, they fell asleep entangled in each other's arms.

CHAPTER FORTY

They slept until past ten the next morning.
Feeling sore and weary Miranda, got up, stretched and headed for the shower. After dressing in jeans and a casual top, she sat on the edge of the couch in the living room of the suite, browsing a brochure of sights to see in Chicago. The Field Museum, the Adler Planetarium, the Shedd Aquarium, the Art Institute.
Parker sat down next to her. "What strikes your fancy?"
Miranda handed him the brochure and sighed. "I don't know. What would you like to do?"
He handed it back. "It's your choice."
"I'd like to go see Jane."
Parker scowled. "We have to let this case go, Miranda."
"I know. But we used to be friends. Maybe we could go see her after sightseeing?"
"We'll see."
Miranda opened the brochure again and turned to the photo of the third tallest building in the US. "I've always wanted to go here. The Willis Building."
"They used to call it the Sears Tower."
"Yeah, I know. I grew up around here, you know."
"And you've never been?"
She gave him a frown. Had he forgotten who her mother was and who she'd been married to?
"Ah, yes. Well, it's high time we remedied that. What do you say we have brunch and then—"
Miranda's cell rang.
She picked it up with a frown. "It's Templeton." She answered it and put it on speaker.
"Steele, have you and Mr. Parker left town yet?" Her voice sounded strange.

"No. He's right here with me. We decided to stay and do some sightseeing. What's wrong?"

"If you have a moment, can you swing by the station? I have someone who's asking for you."

"Who?"

"You wouldn't believe me if I told you. You'll have to see for yourselves."

CHAPTER FORTY-ONE

For once, they skipped breakfast.

They reached the Larrabee station in the scratched and dented Jaguar in thirty minutes, hurried inside, and found Templeton waiting for them in the rear hallway of the Homicide area.

"Come with me."

She led them around the far corner of the cube bank and down a short passage to a different interrogation room.

Templeton opened the door.

Miranda stepped inside and did a double take.

Jane Anderson Prescott was sitting on a folding chair on the far side of a plain metal table. She wore a flannel peach colored running outfit that clashed with her now blotchy skin, though not a highlighted hair on her head was out of place.

A box of tissues sat beside her on the table next to an unopened soft drink can. The tissues she'd used were balled up and covered most of the space in front of her. Her eyes and nose were wet and red.

Stunned, Miranda turned to the detective. "What's going on, Templeton?"

"Mrs. Prescott came to the station around nine o'clock this morning. She said she had a confession to make." Templeton nodded to Jane. "Tell them what you told me."

Jane gave the detective a surly look. "You mean what I've been trying to convince you of all morning?"

"Whatever you want to call it, ma'am."

"Why don't we all sit down." Parker pulled out one of the chairs on the opposite side of the table for Templeton, then did the same for Miranda. He opted to stand.

Miranda slid into the chair and reached across the table. "Jane. What's going on?"

Jane squeezed her hands, then put her own in her lap and stared down at her used tissues. "I came here this morning to tell the detective the truth about Stella and me."

Miranda's shoulders tightened. "We know the truth. She's been arrested."

"Yes. I heard that on the news this morning. That's why I'm here."

She had something to get off her chest. "Okay, tell me."

"I'm not sure how to explain it all again." She reached for another tissue.

Miranda glanced over at Parker. His expression told her he hadn't formed an opinion of all this yet.

"Why don't you start with the day Stella came to see you," Parker said gently. "You said it was about six months ago?"

Jane drew in a breath and pulled herself together. "Yes. I remember that day very clearly. It was early November. I remember the leaves were just starting to fall. It was about ten in the morning. I had just finished a post on my mommy blog, and the doorbell rang. Quinton had gone to work. It was his first day back."

"You mean after he broke his toe?" Miranda said.

Jane nodded. "Yes. The doctor said he wasn't supposed to go into the office for another four weeks, but Quinton said he couldn't stand laying around doing nothing. Even though he had been working from home. He drove himself into the city and said he'd take a cab from the parking garage to the office." She wiped her nose with her tissue. "He couldn't stand not seeing his current love interest, I thought."

Miranda couldn't hide her shock at that comment—or the indifference in Jane's tone.

Current love interest? "You knew about his affairs?"

Jane regarded her with sad brown eyes. "Well, when you're husband comes home with a different perfume on his shirt every few months, it's pretty obvious."

She didn't sound upset about it. More like resigned. It was an old pain she'd been living with for a long time.

"And what did you do about that? When you realized what was going on, I mean."

"Not much, really."

"You just let it go?"

"I wanted to ask him for a divorce. I tried to get up the nerve so many times, but then I'd look at the boys. Whatever else he was, Quinton was a good father. No, he didn't spend much time at home, but what he did he spent with his sons. He certainly didn't spend it with me."

She took a breath, steadied herself and went on.

"Anyway, on that morning in November, I opened the door and there was Stella in all her glory. She had on a faux leopard print coat and hat and deep red lipstick that matched her outfit. I recognized her right away because I'd started to go over old photos from the yearbook for the reunion. I don't think Stella recognized me. I look a lot different from the way I did in high school."

She stared at the wall as if she were reliving the scene.

"Go on," Miranda prompted softly.

Jane shook herself. "Anyway, she asked if she could come in. I said, of course. And then I asked her if she would help with planning the reunion."

"Did she say yes?"

Jane nodded. "Right away. I took her into the kitchen and showed her my plans up to that point. We had coffee and started talking about what we'd been doing since high school. I told her about the boys, and she told me about her three ex-husbands. It was funny. We were like old friends."

Jane and Stella had never been friends in high school.

Jane drew in another breath. "Then Stella reminded me she had been Quinton's steady girl in high school."

"What did you say to that?" She must have expected an affair right away.

"I said I knew that. Stella got nervous and said she had a terrible confession to make."

"A confession?"

Jane nodded. "She told me she had almost cheated on me with Quinton. She'd gone to a hotel for a night of 'hot sex,' as she put it, but he hadn't shown up."

"He stood her up."

"That's what she thought. I told her Quinton had just broken his toe."

"How did she react to that?"

"She seemed a little stunned."

Miranda bet she was. She'd realized if she hadn't gone to Jane's house and confessed, she could have kept on having an affair with him and gotten that hot sex.

"And then she said there were others he'd actually gone to bed with."

So now it was time to get that revenge. Stella was probably mad at Prescott for not contacting her and telling her about his toe. Or maybe she sensed it was over between them at that point.

"I told her I knew and that I had been putting up with Quinton's affairs for years. I was going to divorce him, but then I thought of the boys. I decided I would wait until my sons were grown. I broke down in tears. And then..." She reached for a tissue. "It's funny. I don't really know how it all came together. It was all about having a nice life now, and payback, and that I deserved better."

She blew her nose.

Miranda glanced at Templeton. The detective's face was unreadable. "What are you talking about, Jane?"

"We—Stella and I—we decided we were going to get rid of Quinton."

"Get rid of him?"

"We were going to kill him," she said, as if it were the most logical thing in the world.

Miranda thought the floor had shifted under her chair and she was about to fall through a deep hole.

Jane Anderson had plotted her husband's murder with Stella La Stella? That couldn't be right.

"Quinton had a large insurance policy," Jane explained. "I told Stella we could split it. Stella said she'd only need a third. She said I'd need more to take care of the boys."

Miranda held up a hand. Her brain was spinning. Jane told Stella about the insurance policy, and Jane was going to split it with her? Three million dollars? And Stella didn't want to take it all?

This was insane. But she had to let Jane tell the rest of it. "Okay. What happened next?"

"We did research."

"Research?"

"On how to kill someone."

And get away with it, she meant.

"First we looked at poisons. That was the most obvious choice. We did the research on my computer, since Stella used hers at the television station. She was so careful. She insisted I erase the history every time we used it."

But a computer history could be recovered. Surely Stella knew that. She was making Jane leave all the evidence. Making her look like the guilty one.

"We thought about hiring someone, but that seemed too risky. We thought about staging a suicide in our home, but I didn't want one of the boys to find him. Finally, we decided we'd give him an overdose of oxycodone, since Quinton already had a prescription for his toe. He hadn't taken much. He didn't like drugs. He was due for a refill by then, and I went to pick it up. It wasn't easy to get, but I managed. Anyway, we decided the best way to do it was to grind up some pills, put them in his drink, and then get him to drive somewhere. He'd get in an accident and it would all seem as if he'd done it to himself."

Pretty good plan. Except that wasn't how it played out at all.

"Stella came over to the house one afternoon with a mortar and pestle. She took six of the oxycodone pills from Quinton's refill and ground them up. Then I found one of Quinton's empty echinacea oil bottles and she put the powder in there. Stella said it was best if she kept the refill bottle so Quinton wouldn't find it. The next step was for her to get in touch with Quinton and ask to have drinks with him in town one night the following week. He was driving regularly now instead of taking the train. So they'd go somewhere, have dinner, and she'd slip the ground drugs into his martini. Quinton always drank dry martinis at dinner. He was predictable that way."

"But that's not what happened."

"No."

Miranda waited.

Jane reached for the soft drink can, opened it, and took a sip. She looked down at it as if she wished it were something stronger. Then she drew in another breath and continued.

"Stella and I had been spending a lot of time together. A lot of it was planning for the reunion party. Keira and Keely were at the house, too. We had a lot of dinners together while we were working. When Quinton learned Stella and I were getting close, I guess he thought she had told me about the hotel. And probably his other affairs." She laughed softly as she wiped a tear away. "I suppose he thought he had kept them from me all these years. Maybe he thought I was too stupid to notice. But one night when Stella and the others weren't at the house, he came home early and confessed everything. He told me he'd been cheating on me for years. He said he thought he had a sex problem. He wanted to go into therapy. He said he realized what he'd been throwing away, and he wanted to fix it. If I'd have him, he wanted to make our marriage work."

Miranda sat back at that one. Quinton Prescott, corporate playboy wanted to fix his marriage? "Did you believe him?"

"Yes. He'd never said anything like that before. And he did what he said. We started to mend things. We went to counseling. He started to look for another job, one where he wouldn't have to work such long hours. He thought about opening his own practice. We planned a trip to Europe next summer."

She folded her hands on the table and sat quietly for a long moment.

"What did Stella say about all this? Did you tell her?"

"Yes, I did. She was happy for me. Thrilled, in fact. She said she wished things could have worked out that way for her with one of her husbands."

"And what about your plans to kill Quinton?"

Jane frowned as if the answer was perfectly obvious. "We changed our minds, of course."

Oh, yeah? "What happened to the ground up oxycodone?"

"Stella told me she flushed it down the toilet."

Convenient. But she kept the rest of the bottle.

"So you see, as I've been trying to explain to Detective Templeton, Stella is innocent. Yes, we plotted to kill him, but we didn't go through with it."

Stella sure had Jane twisted around her little finger. It was plain to Miranda what had happened.

When Jane and Prescott got back together, Stella felt more betrayed than ever. Jane might have dropped the plan to kill her husband, but Stella hadn't. She just changed the method.

"Jane, if you believe Stella is innocent, how do you think your husband died?"

"I don't know. Didn't the police say it was an accident at first?"

"He had oxycodone in his system."

She blinked in surprise. She hadn't known that. "I don't know how that happened."

"Stella's fingerprints were found on his tie."

Now she nearly came out of the chair. "What?"

"Stella's fingerprints. On the tie." The tie that he'd been hanged with.

Jane pressed a hand to her head as if she thought she was going crazy. "I—that can't be. There must be some mistake." She turned to Templeton. "Aren't you going to let Stella go? I've told you what really happened."

Templeton stiffened. "I'm sorry, Mrs. Prescott. I can't do that. There's too much evidence against her."

"But she didn't do it. We decided not to kill him."

Templeton didn't answer. She simply rose and moved to the door.

Desperation in her eyes, Jane turned to Miranda. "You'll have to help me then, Miranda. You and your husband. I want to hire you to prove Stella is innocent. Will you take my case?"

Miranda glanced over at Parker. She could tell he was stunned, though he didn't let it show.

"We'll have to get back to you about that, Jane," he told her as he got to his feet.

Miranda rose as well. "He's right. We need to talk this over."

CHAPTER FORTY-TWO

As she exited the interrogation room, Miranda's head was spinning. "I need some air."

She pushed past Templeton and headed for the back door.

Parker followed her with Templeton beside him.

Outside in the parking lot, she hugged herself pacing back and forth along the short walkway. She stared out at the rows of squad cars parked along the fence near the bare trees.

This was nuts. How could Jane have plotted Prescott's murder with Stella La Stella, his old girlfriend? And yet it all made sense in some crazy kind of way.

"Are you all right?" Parker said quietly at her side.

She rubbed her arms. She'd run out without her coat and she was chilled, but she couldn't go back inside yet.

"Do you believe her? Do you think Stella's innocent?"

"It's highly unlikely after that chase up I-94 last night."

He was still angry about that. Not just because of what she'd done to the Jag. Because the bitch had shot at her. It had reminded him too much of Boston. Just as it had her.

She paced a little more. "Jane wants us to prove Stella's innocent. Hah. We need to wake Jane up. We need to prove that bitch is guilty." She glanced over at Templeton.

The detective was quiet and wore a troubled expression on her square-shaped face.

A feeling of apprehension came over Miranda. "What are you going to do with her?"

"With Mrs. Prescott?"

"Of course, with Mrs. Prescott."

"I'm sorry, Steele. I have to hold her. According to her statement, she's an accomplice."

"But she said she changed her mind. She said she and Prescott were getting back together."

"The evidence doesn't support that."

So Templeton thought they had made up the other story, the one Jane just told them about giving up the idea of getting rid of Prescott. She believed the rest of it.

Miranda spun around to Parker. "We need to get a confession from Stella. She needs to exonerate Jane." She reached for Templeton's arm. "Do you still have her here?"

She nodded. "We're holding her in a cell. She's meeting with her lawyer."

"Can we talk to her?"

"Let me see." With a grimace, Templeton stepped away and pulled out her phone to make a call.

Probably to the guard.

She talked for several minutes, then hung up and turned back to Miranda. "The lawyer's okayed a meeting, but he'll be in the room with you."

Best they could get for now. "Good enough. Thanks."

"It's this way."

CHAPTER FORTY-THREE

Templeton led them back inside, through a door on the other side of the cube bank and down two sets of metal stairs. After passing several doors on either side, she stopped at one and swiped her badge at the lock.

It buzzed, the door clicked, and she pushed it open.

With Parker close behind her, Miranda entered the cold little room. It had a hard metal table, matching chairs, and gray cinder block walls. Recalling days in her past when she had been arrested, she eyed the camera in the corner of the ceiling.

The three of them remained standing for another ten minutes.

At last, the door buzzed again, and a large guard entered leading the prisoner and a tall, pear-shaped man in a dark suit.

Dressed in an orange jumpsuit, Stella glared at her inquisitors as she took a seat at the table. She wore no makeup. Her face was pale, and her dark hair was flat, lacking its usual luster.

If she didn't know better, Miranda wouldn't have recognized her.

The tall man stuck out a hand. "I'm Oscar Perino. Ms. La Stella's representation."

Miranda wanted to kick the man, but she shook hands instead.

Parker was more civil. "Thank you for meeting with us, Mr. Perino."

"I have to inform you I've advised my client not to answer questions."

"A reasonable approach." Parker gestured to the table as if the lawyer was a guest at his mansion. "Shall we sit down and discuss it?"

Miranda slid into a chair and studied the man's long wavy iron gray hair, beak like nose, and horn rimmed half glasses.

"My client maintains her innocence in this matter."

"We understand that." Miranda said, looking at Stella.

Stella kept her eyes on the surface of the table.

Might as well get things started. "We've come to tell your client that Jane came to make a confession this morning."

Stella came alive, her piercing blue eyes popping open. "Jane did? What did she say?"

Perino leaned over to her. "Ms. La Stella, please let me do the talking."

Miranda honed in on Stella. "She told us everything."

"Everything?"

"Ms. La Stella," Perino warned. "Don't say any more."

Stella ignored him. She pounded her fists on the table. "No, no, no. I told her not to do that. I can take care of myself. She's got the boys to think of."

Perino cleared his throat. "Ms. La Stella—"

Stella waved him away.

Perino sat back and shook his head.

Miranda kept her gaze on Stella. "Why did you pretend to be her friend?"

"I didn't pretend."

"You never liked her in high school. You used to trip her in the hall and knock books out of her hands."

"I was a different person back then."

"But you and Prescott were a number, right?"

"You know that."

"And you wanted to be a number again. Until he stood you up last November."

"I've already told you that."

"And so you found a way to get close to him. To get close to his wife. To manipulate her and talk her into paying him back for his infidelities. Right?"

Stella sat back with her mouth open. "I'm not a homewrecker. What Quinton and I had was in the past. I discovered I didn't even like the guy any more."

Oh, that was rich. "I thought you said you fell back in love with him."

"That was before I went to his home. Before I got to know Jane and his kids."

"You're saying you had a sudden change of heart?"

"That's right."

Shaking her head, Miranda sat back in her chair. She couldn't believe the gall of this woman. "You know what I think, Stella? I think you were livid when Prescott decided to give up his philandering and start being faithful to Jane. You had been hoping to kill him and pin the murder on her. But suddenly, she backed out. That's when you came up with the plan to pay both of them back by killing him at the reunion party."

Stella let out a stunned laugh. "That's ridiculous."

Perino raised a finger and finally got a word in. "I'd have to agree."

Miranda ignored him. "Didn't you talk to him on the terrace just before the contest winners were announced?"

Stella glared at her. "No."

"We have a witness who saw you."

"Your witness is a liar."

"Your fingerprints were found on Prescott's tie. You know. The white silk one we found him hanging by."

Stella sat back, opened her mouth, closed it again.

Perino closed his eyes as if in prayer. "Please, Ms. La Stella. I beg you. Do not say anything else."

But Stella seemed to be in another world. "Okay, Miranda. You're right. I did talk to Quinton on the terrace."

Finally. Miranda leaned in again. "And he told you to leave him alone, right? Because you were stalking him."

She laughed and shook her head. "I started doing that in high school. The thing with Quinton's tie. He always wore a suit and tie on the days there were student council meetings. If I thought he was getting out of line, I'd grab the end of his tie, shake my finger at him, and tell him to straighten up."

Really. "And that's what you did on the terrace?"

"He was drunk. Really drunk. And babbling about not being good enough for Jane. I took him by the tie and told him he better straighten up and make good on the promises he'd made her. 'Quinton,' I said, 'you've got a good thing going. Don't mess it up because of your dick'."

Perino put his head in his hands.

They were close. So close. "What did Prescott say to that?"

Stella lifted a shoulder. "He mumbled something. I think he said he couldn't help himself."

What a crock. Miranda folded her arms. "Try again."

"It's true. All I could think of was how trusting Jane was. How it would break her heart if things didn't work out for them. It upset me so much, I broke into tears. I had to go to the ladies room to pull myself together."

"Is that when you decided to put oxycodone in Prescott's drink?"

"What?"

"The oxycodone pills from Prescott's prescription that you ground up at his house with Jane. She said you put them in a bottle and took it with you. You were supposed to have drinks with Prescott in the city and slip it into his martini. You didn't flush that powder down the toilet, after all. Did you?"

Stella's chest began to heave as if she were having trouble breathing. She looked around the room, at the faces staring at her, demanding answers. She glanced up at the camera and winced.

Then she turned to her lawyer. "You were right, Oscar. I shouldn't have said anything. Take me back to my cell."

CHAPTER FORTY-FOUR

"I'm sorry about how this has turned out," Templeton said.

They were standing at the detective's cube, still reeling from their interviews.

"Me, too." Miranda tapped her fingers on the top of the cube wall.

She couldn't believe how easily Stella had wormed her way into Jane's life. How she'd gotten her to agree to murder her husband. How she'd made it all seem like an accident. She probably hoped the police would find evidence in Jane's house and arrest her. If only Jane hadn't been so trusting. If only she hadn't come to the station today to try to save Stella.

It couldn't be that easy. Stella had to have left something behind that incriminated her.

Miranda looked at Parker, but couldn't read his face.

Determined to do something, she turned back to Templeton. "There might be some evidence in Jane's house. Something we overlooked the first time we searched it."

Templeton gave her a strained look. "I'm not authorized to continue the investigation, Steele."

"But you've got an innocent woman in there." She waved her hand toward the room where she assumed Jane was still sitting. "What are you going to do with her?"

"We're waiting for the DA's review of her case. Once that's done, we'll book her on a felony murder charge."

"Felony murder?"

"She was there when La Stella killed Prescott at the reunion party. By all the evidence, she was part of the setup."

"You're going to put her in jail? She's got kids, Templeton."

Templeton looked down at her feet, obviously feeling guilty. "I spoke to Jane's mother earlier. She's willing to take care of the kids for now."

Miranda felt like she had been punched in the chest. "Can we talk to Jane again? She did hire us as investigators."

Templeton hesitated, her pursed lips going back and forth. Finally, she nodded and took them back down the hall.

Miranda didn't tell Jane about their interview with Stella. All she said was that she and Parker wanted to get another look at her house and asked for her keys.

Jane looked up at MIranda with her big brown eyes. "Does that mean you're taking my case?"

"That's still to be determined," Parker told her firmly.

They grabbed their coats and headed out.

Back outside, Miranda hurried across the parking lot to the sorry looking Jag. Anger prickled through her as she remembered the high speed chase Stella had put them through last night. Before she could reach for the door handle, someone shouted at her.

She turned and saw the same news reporter that had accosted her the other day.

The woman hurried over and stuck her microphone in Miranda's face. "Ms. Steele, you've been working closely with the police. What can you tell us about the death of attorney Quinton Prescott?"

"Nothing," Miranda snapped, barely suppressing a growl.

The reporter wasn't fazed by her tone. "Someone has been arrested."

They already knew that and had reported the details that morning.

"You'll have to speak to the police about the matter," Parker told the woman, wedging himself between her and Miranda.

She was undaunted. "The police haven't been forthcoming about the matter. Why hasn't Sergeant Demarco made a formal statement yet?"

"You'll have to ask him. You'll find the entrance on the other side of that building." Parker indicated the police station behind them.

When the reporters turned to look at it, he bustled Miranda into the car, hurried around the dented hood, and got inside.

He had to tap the horn to make them get out of the way once he started the car. It took them a minute to move, but at last the Jag rolled out of the lot and turned onto the street.

Parker waited until they were half a block away, then spoke in a low restrained tone. "Are you sure you want to continue this investigation, Miranda?" He seemed upset.

"Don't you?"

"We are supposed to be retired."

And this case wasn't supposed to go on this long. But what else could they do?

She shook her head. "We can't let them put Jane in jail. She didn't do anything."

"She plotted her husband's murder with Stella."

Miranda couldn't believe he'd said that. "Quinton Prescott was a no-good, low-down cheating bastard."

"I'm not excusing his behavior. It's reprehensible. But in the eyes of the police, it does give Jane motive."

"But she changed her mind about getting rid of Prescott. I don't think she would have had the nerve to go through with it, anyway. We have to prove this was all Stella's doing."

Parker let out a slow breath as they rolled over the Chicago River. "What if we don't find anything to do that?"

And that was likely. They'd already been to the house. Still, her heart was breaking for her friend. "I don't know, Parker."

Parker was silent as they passed the Tribune building and turned onto Halsted. He stole a glance at Miranda and saw heartbreak and determination on her lovely face. That passion for justice that had made him fall in love with her.

But this case?

He understood her desire to help her friend, but they had been through hell and survived. They had decided to give up this work. It had been her idea. To Parker, continuing this investigation felt like they were tempting Fate.

And yet, he couldn't say no to her.

He reached across the seat and took her hand. "Let's give it one more day. If we can't find anything, we'll let the police take over. Agreed?"

The surprise on her face warmed his heart.

And then she smiled at him and nodded. "Agreed."

CHAPTER FORTY-FIVE

They went through every room of Jane's now empty house.

The living room, the den, the white kitchen with all the cabinets, Quinton Prescott's exercise room where he'd broken his toe. Then they headed for the walnut staircase.

Upstairs they re-examined the boys' rooms and the hall closet. Once again, Parker took the master bedroom while Miranda went through the master bath.

As she stood staring at the bottle of oxycodone in the medicine cabinet, she thought of Prescott's text messages she'd read through yesterday.

Not one of them was to Jane.

There was nothing at all to prove they were getting back together. It was hard for her to believe it, herself.

She gave up and went down the hall.

She found Parker in a small room that had been turned into an office. He had found Jane's laptop and used some fancy manipulations to unerase the history she and Stella had deleted.

"It's all here, just as she said." His voice was ominous.

Miranda came and looked over his shoulder.

She scanned the list of sites on ricin and belladonna, pesticides and laundry products. Most of the pages were about oxycodone.

"Just as she said," Miranda echoed as she sank into a white wooden chair with a pink ruffled cushion.

"I'm not finding any evidence she changed her mind in her emails, either." Parker's voice sounded far away.

So far they'd only incriminated Jane more. Miranda put a hand to her forehead, trying to push back a headache.

"I'm feeling foggy," she said just as her stomach growled.

Parker glanced at the time on the screen. He turned off the laptop and rose. "You haven't had breakfast or lunch, and it's past three o'clock. I've been derelict of my primary duty."

Feeding her, he meant.

He stretched a hand out to her and pulled her up and out of the chair.

"Okay, I'm up." She supposed they had to eat. There wasn't anything to find here.

They headed out of the room and down the lovely staircase.

What to do next? She couldn't think of a thing. "Do you want to get something nearby?"

He took her arm as they stepped through the foyer. "Why don't we have lunch at the Royal Rose Hotel?"

She brightened. "And afterwards, check out the terrace again?"

"That's what I had in mind."

Her hopes rose as she took in his dazzling smile. "Did I ever tell you what a brilliant PI you are?"

"And you are, too. When you're fed."

"Then we'd better eat right away."

And she turned to give him a kiss before they hurried out the door.

CHAPTER FORTY-SIX

The main restaurant in the Royal Rose was on the nineteenth level, one floor down from the reception hall where the class reunion party had taken place.

All clean lines and elegant atmosphere, it featured an off-white decor with lighted columns, tall glass vases of fresh flowers, and meticulously trimmed bonsai plants. Plus they could see Michigan Avenue through the twenty-foot windows they had been seated beside.

They started with a delicate Caesar salad made of hearts of romaine, pancetta, and parmesan, and moved on to jumbo prawn cocktails. Finally they indulged in King Salmon with snap peas and baby zucchini, and Chilean Sea Bass with summer squash and asparagus in a champagne sabayon.

Miranda moaned when the flavorful mustardy sauce hit her tongue, and then finished everything on her plate. She'd been hungrier than she realized after getting off Parker's normal feeding schedule for her.

Parker scanned a menu. "They have some lovely dessert offerings. Pineapple coconut, Mandarin Hazelnut."

Miranda rubbed her stomach. It sounded wonderful, but she didn't have room. "I don't know how I'm going to get out of this chair, much less investigate a crime scene."

He put the menu down. "But you will, won't you."

"You know me only too well."

He paid the bill, and they made their way to the elevator and rode up a floor.

They passed through the golden hallway and stopped at the entrance of the banquet hall.

Miranda peeked through the doors.

Gone were the banners, posters, and yearbook photos on the wall. The round tables had been replaced by rows of rectangular ones facing large screens near the front. There was a podium with a microphone. Some group was having a meeting here soon.

She didn't see any staff members. The whole place was empty and quiet.

"Let's make ourselves at home," she whispered to Parker.

"Just what I was about to suggest."

Moving behind the tables, Miranda made a beeline across the room to the set of tall glass doors on the opposite side.

She pointed to the pair on the left. "This was where we entered the terrace, right?"

"As I recall." Parker opened the door for her, and they stepped out onto the terrazzo floor of the large rectangular space.

The wind was brisk, and she could hear the noisy traffic on the street below as she strolled to the spot where she'd stood making out with Parker last Saturday night.

"This is where we were."

Parker moved next to her and took her in his arms. "Just an inch or two over this way, I believe." He turned her a bit and took a step closer.

He drank her in with his intense gray eyes, making her shiver all over.

She slipped her arms around his neck and wished they could go back to that night, wished it had turned out differently.

But it hadn't.

"This is right." She turned her head and pointed. "And I saw Prescott talking with Donahue right over there."

Parker focused on the spot. "Exactly."

She let go of Parker and eyed the marble tabletops, the white cotton canvas loveseats, and the clear Plexiglas banister with its brushed silver guardrail.

Starting down the aisle, she counted the loveseat ensembles and stopped when she was near the other end of the terrace.

She pointed down at a couch. "This is about where Prescott was sitting when Donahue saw him out here."

Parker came up beside her. "A good enough estimate."

"Prescott invites Donahue to have a drink with him. Donahue says no and comes over here." She stepped over to the banister.

The Plexiglass was clean and shiny. There were no fingerprints now.

"Prescott gets up and joins him there." Again Parker moved to her side.

"Prescott is drunk, slurring his speech. Donahue gets disgusted with him and leaves. Maybe through there." She pointed to one of the glass doors on this end of the terrace.

"But not before Prescott mentions 'woman trouble' and indicates someone is stalking him."

"Right." She thought a moment. "I didn't see Stella come out to the terrace, did you?"

"Not at that time."

"So let's assume she came in the doors that Donahue exited."

"Again, a reasonable assumption."

Miranda put a finger to her chin and eyed a marble table in the corner of the terrace. It would have been in shadows that night. "That's where Victoria Winslow might have been standing when she saw Stella with Prescott."

"It would give her a good view of the couple," Parker agreed. "And Victoria would have been close enough to hear their conversation."

Miranda pointed at Parker. "Prescott was swilling down dry martinis in those fancy colored glasses."

"According to Donahue."

"Stella would have had to have grabbed one from one of the servers."

"Or gotten it from the bar."

"Right. She would have to pour the ground oxycodone into the drink without anyone noticing. Where could she have done that?"

Considering the question for a moment, Parker peered through the glass doors. "There were plenty of dark spots inside the reception hall. With everyone drinking and dancing, no one would have noticed."

Still it seemed odd. Miranda stepped over to the glass doors and pretended to come through them with a martini in her hand.

"So Stella hands Prescott a glass and he downs it, already too blitzed to notice it was spiked."

She mimicked the action.

Parker pretended to drink the contents of the imaginary glass in one gulp. He grimaced. "It has a bitter taste, but it works almost immediately."

He knew from experience.

She ran through Victoria's testimony as they acted out the rest.

"Stella touches Prescott's arm. He jerks away. She tells him to get some coffee. He tells her not to make a scene. Prescott accuses Stella of stalking him, tells her she's a sick woman."

"And according to Ms. Winslow, that was when everyone started back into the reception hall."

Miranda frowned. "Guess that included us. I didn't see anything like that going on over here. Did you?"

"No, but there were other people between us. And we were otherwise occupied."

Right. Parker's kisses could make her oblivious to almost anything.

She pointed at the doors again. "Victoria said she went out through one of the rear doors, turned back, and saw Stella and Prescott still standing here. So now's Stella's chance." Miranda peered over the banister. "This is the spot where you and the two football players pulled him back over, right?"

"Yes," Parker said darkly.

"Okay. By now, Prescott's buzzed out of his mind. He's standing here swaying back and forth. Maybe he leans over the banister."

"You'll excuse me if I don't go through those motions."

Ignoring the comment, Miranda shook her head. She peered over the banister at the street far below. "Hmm…"

Parker caught her drift. He stated it out loud first. "If Prescott had simply fallen over the wall, or been pushed, it would have been difficult to prove murder."

"Why tie him with the tie then?"

Parker's brow creased as he considered the question. "Perhaps Stella thought he'd suffer more that way. Or perhaps it was so she could watch him die, if she has a sadistic nature."

Miranda scratched at her hair. Why wouldn't watching his body hit the sidewalk twenty stories below be enough? Especially if she'd originally planned for him to die in a car wreck.

Something wasn't right about that.

"Anyway." Alongside the railing Miranda bent over at the waist. "Maybe Prescott's about to upchuck from his buzz, so he leans over like this."

"And Stella takes the opportunity to tie the end of his tie to the railing." Parker mimicked the action, now playing Stella's part.

"He might have leaned over the banister then, and she just gave him a little push."

"If he was inebriated enough, he might think he was climbing into bed."

"And over he went." She gestured into the air, paused, then tapped her chin with her finger. "But if Stella wanted to watch, she didn't have time. She was supposed to be with Jane and the others at the podium. She'd been crying, so she had to head to the ladies room and clean herself up first."

Miranda turned around, moved to the glass doors once more, and peered through them.

"Everyone's attention was on Jane at the podium," Parker said coming up behind her. "No one noticed her in the back of the room."

"Maybe there was another way to the ladies room." Miranda rubbed her arms. Then she turned her head and saw something she hadn't noticed before. "Look at that."

The Plexiglas banister made a ninety degree turn at the terrace's corner, but it ran only about two-thirds of the way back to the reception hall. Between the hall and the banister was a solid gray wall. There was a door in the wall painted the same shade, making it semi-hidden.

Miranda stepped over to it. "What's this door used for?"

"Let's find out." Parker reached around her, found a hidden handle, and opened it.

A light came on and they stepped into a stairwell.

She studied the space a moment. With metal steps and handrails, it looked like the one at the police station.

"Let's find out where it goes."

Starting down, they descended seven steps to a small concrete landing. They went down another seven steps and found another door. The smell of food was in the air, and Miranda could hear clanging and clattering. She opened the door a crack and peeked inside.

"It's a kitchen."

"The kitchen to the restaurant where we ate."

"This must be where they prepared the appetizers for the reunion party upstairs. The servers used the stairs to deliver them to the guests."

"That appears to be the way the operation works."

Okay, so what did that have to do with anything?

Folding her arms, she tapped her foot and studied the small space. Another stairwell descended into darkness below. A narrow window about three feet high let in light from the outside. There was nothing below the window but gray cinder blocks. Nothing on the floor.

Suddenly a strange sensation slithered down her back. A sensation she'd felt before.

But what did it mean? There was nothing here.

Wait.

She pointed down. "What's that?"

Parker moved over to the far corner of the landing just below the window. He bent down.

She followed him. "Is that what I think it is?"

"It's a small plastic bottle."

Clear plastic. Wedged in the corner, it looked like the kind you put shampoo or mouthwash in for travel.

"I need to get a shot of that." Miranda reached for her phone and took several photos of the container in the corner, then of the stairwell and the door to the kitchen for context.

Parker pulled a handkerchief from his pocket and carefully lifted the bottle from the floor. "It appears to have some powder residue."

Miranda craned her neck to peer at it more closely. It sure did. "White powder residue."

"I'd say we need to get this to Detective Templeton right away."

She nodded. "I would agree. Like now."

Gingerly he slipped the bottle into his pocket, they headed back up to the terrace, and made their way out of the Royal Rose Hotel.

CHAPTER FORTY-SEVEN

"The bottle you brought in contained oxycodone residue, all right." Holding up the lab report, Kadera peeked over the wall of the double cube where Miranda and Parker had worked the past two days.

They had been sitting there for half an hour waiting for results.

When they had reached the police station, they'd learned Templeton was in the field on another case, and Demarco was at a meeting at headquarters, so Kadera had bagged the bottle, taken it down to the lab, and disappeared.

Miranda sat up in her chair. "Were there any fingerprints on the bottle?"

Kadera gave her a sly grin. "A partial."

"Really?" A jolt of excitement shot through her.

"Yep. It's pretty clear, too. The lab's working on matching it to Ms. La Stella."

Miranda stared at Kadera, hardly able to believe his words. Then she heard Parker's low voice behind her.

"What if it doesn't match?"

She spun around. "It has to match Stella." Didn't it?

Kadera shrugged. "Then they'll try to match it to Mrs. Prescott."

"There won't be a match there." No way Jane could have dropped the bottle in that stairwell. She'd been at the podium.

"If there's no hit with them, the lab techs will go through the guests at the reunion party one by one."

One by one? Miranda's stomach tightened. "How long do you think that will take?"

Kadera shrugged. "Depends on what they find. Could be a few hours. Could be tomorrow morning."

Miranda's brows rose. Tomorrow morning? John Fry back at the Agency could match that print in an hour. But then, he didn't have a whole police district's work on his plate.

No, it wouldn't take that long. That print had to match Stella.

Kadera danced from foot to foot as if to say, why don't you two find something else to do.

Parker took the hint and rose. "I'd say it's a good time to do that sightseeing."

Miranda didn't want to leave. They could have results any minute.

But then she looked at Parker's outstretched hand and decided to humor him. He had been patient with her. She owed him.

She took his hand and let him pull her to her feet. "Okay. I'm game."

CHAPTER FORTY-EIGHT

They headed back to the hotel to change into casual clothes and comfortable shoes.

It was too late in the day for a tour bus, so Parker suggested a stroll along the riverwalk on foot. Since the weather was a little warmer, Miranda thought that was a good idea.

Hand in hand they ambled along, taking in the green water, the yellow river taxis, and the varied city architecture, which included the Marina Towers, the Wrigley Building, and the McCormick Bridgehouse.

Then they hopped in a cab and headed south to the Art Institute.

As the taxi pulled up to the majestic building, Parker turned to her with concern on his handsome face. "Miranda, are you sure this is where you want to go?"

She knew why he was worried. Tannenburg had attended the School of the Art Institute, and this was where they'd first learned about him last fall.

Normally that would be enough to keep her far away from the place, even though they weren't going to the school now. And she certainly wasn't an art connoisseur.

But as she stared up at the huge green lions keeping watch before the flags and arches of the massive neoclassical facade, something scratched at the back of her neck. That strange, prickly feeling she often had when a case was about to break.

The same feeling she'd had earlier in the stairwell of the Royal Rose Hotel.

She had to find out why.

Confidently she nodded. "I'm sure."

They got out of the cab and went inside.

It wasn't until they had traversed the lobby and she was climbing the endless echoing steps of the Greek style atrium, moving toward a dark statute of a headless nude, that Miranda felt another sensation.

She stopped cold in the middle of the steps.

Parker reached for her arm. "What is it?"

"I don't know. I think I had a flashback."

"What sort of flashback?"

She stared at the statue and remembered a field trip she'd gone on when she was a high school freshman.

She could see her classmates climbing these very steps. Stella and Prescott had just started dating. They were ascending the steps hand in hand. A girl Stella was jealous of followed right behind them. Stella tripped the girl and made her fall. She cut her chin open on one of the steps. She started to bleed on the marble, and the teacher had gone berserk. The tour guide had to give the girl first aid.

Miranda didn't think the girl was Jane. She couldn't remember who it was.

And she didn't want to muddy their time together with something that might not mean anything.

She shook it off. "It's nothing. C'mon. I'll race you up these stairs."

They took in all the famous pieces. The American Gothic, Andy Warhol's silkscreen of Liz Taylor, Hopper's all night diner, and the huge late nineteenth century Seurat depicting people in a park in Paris with tiny dots.

And then it was closing time.

"Would you like to get something to eat?" Parker asked as they stood outside on the concrete steps behind the big green lions.

The sun had set, and once again the city was aglow with light.

She shook her head. "I'm still full from that enormous lunch you fed me."

"Shall we try the Willis Tower then?"

She checked her phone. No text. "You haven't heard from Kadera, have you?"

"No, I haven't." He would have told her right away.

Letting out a sigh, she thought of Kadera's words. The police were busy. They might not have even started to match that fingerprint yet. It would probably take until tomorrow to get the results.

She took Parker's hand and smiled at him. "Yeah, I'd like that."

"The Willis Tower it is, then."

They caught another cab and took it to what was once the tallest building in the world.

CHAPTER FORTY-NINE

The cab dropped them off in front of the gleaming, hundred-and-ten-story skyscraper on West Wacker Drive that stretched into the blackness of the night like a beacon.

They took the elevator to floor 103, their ears popping as they traveled over twenty-four feet per second, according to the automated tour voice.

When the doors opened, Parker guided Miranda to the tall windows facing east, and she took in the dazzling lights of the city far below. The tall skyscrapers looked like Monopoly tokens, and she could make out the prominent landmarks. The planetarium, the aquarium, the dark mass of Lake Michigan. The tiny lights out there that must have been boats.

It was a lovely scene, but she had little taste for ships and bodies of water after Boston. Instead her mind went back to Jane.

Suddenly she realized something.

She turned to Parker. "The fingerprint on the bottle we found at the hotel can't be Stella's."

Parker's brow rose in disapproval. He didn't like that she'd been thinking about the case, no matter how hard he'd tried to distract her. "What makes you say that, other than the length of time it's taking the police to process it?"

"Where we found it. The killer wouldn't have left it in that back stairwell on purpose. And Stella went to the ladies room and then joined Jane at the podium."

"Unless she took a short detour downstairs."

"So you're saying she did leave it there on purpose?"

"I'm saying we should wait until the police tell us whose print is on the bottle." Parker took her hand and led her to another view while a new group of sightseers took their place.

They moved to a set of windows overlooking the north side of the city.

A young boy pointed in the distance. "Look, Mama. De ball park."

He was excited about seeing the lighted outline of Wrigley Field.

Miranda had to smile.

Then her smile faded as she thought again of Prescott dangling from the banister over the city. Poor Jane. They must have her in a holding cell now.

Something wasn't right about where they found that bottle, but she couldn't put her finger on it. Irritated with herself, she let out a breath.

She had to let it go.

The truth would come out. The police would release Jane eventually.

She glanced over at Parker and saw the lines in his face.

He was worried about her. He hadn't really wanted to be involved in this case. Her getting shot at yesterday had been a stark reminder of watching her fall on that fish pier in Boston. They were too close to that experience. They needed distance. They were supposed to be retired.

He could see what she was thinking, but he smiled at her tenderly. "I think you'll like this."

"What is it?"

"Come and see."

He led her around a corner to a transparent box that jutted out from the building about four feet. It was made entirely of Plexiglass, and its see-through floor was held in place by thick cables.

"Can we go out there?"

"It's part of the attraction."

A group moved out of the box and Parker gestured for her to enter.

She stepped inside, and her heart surged with a dizzying thrill as lights one-hundred and three stories directly below her feet came into view.

"This is cool, Parker."

"It is."

A tall person could stand comfortably inside this box, and Parker fit nicely.

She gazed out and felt another rush in her stomach as she took in the vista of the vast city at night. The buildings and streets down below created a distinctive pattern. Straight lines of lights seemed to move toward each other across the black surface, all the way out to the western suburbs. A design worthy of the Art Institute, she thought.

And suddenly she remembered the dream she'd had in the hospital in Lake Placid over a year and a half ago.

Her brother, a Polynesian fire dancer, had shown her her life and the places where she'd grown up. She'd believed he'd been showing her her destiny.

But was it?

What was the use of a destiny like that if it meant putting the ones you love at risk? And putting old friends in jail for a cheater?

Parker touched her shoulder. "Our time's up."

She came out of her reverie. "Okay. Yeah."

As she stepped out of the box, she nearly bumped into a woman in a frumpy coat.

"I'm sorry. I didn't mean to—" Miranda scanned her sharp features, her dark hair and eyes. She recognized her. "Ms. Winslow?"

Shyly, the woman smiled. "Victoria, please. We did go to high school together, after all." Her voice had that soft refined lilt Miranda remembered.

"Victoria," Miranda repeated.

She didn't know what to say to her. She wanted to ask what the woman was doing here.

Victoria anticipated the question. "I come up here occasionally when I'm on break from the restaurant. I just can't get enough of this view. It gives a person perspective. Don't you think?"

"I guess it does."

Parker was at her side now. "Good evening, Victoria."

"Good evening, Mr. Parker." She leaned in close to Miranda and lowered her voice. "I heard on the news Stella was—arrested last night."

Miranda nodded. "Yes, she was."

"It was a terrible thing, but I'm glad I could help."

"Your testimony was helpful," Parker said.

"I'm glad." She smiled sadly, then studied Miranda with an odd look. "Well, I'll let you both be. I have to get back. Have a good evening."

"You, too."

She turned and hurried toward the exit.

"Strange woman," Parker murmured beside her.

"She always was that way." Feeling as sorry for her as she had in high school, Miranda watched Victoria's drab coat disappear behind the elevator doors.

CHAPTER FIFTY

They stopped at a bistro and had a late dinner of oysters and steak kabobs with lime wasabi sauce.

When they got back to the hotel, Miranda felt spent. She headed for the shower, but when she emerged from the bathroom, she didn't feel much better.

Parker brushed her cheek with his lips on his way to the shower.

She held onto him a moment, relishing his touch.

They should have showered together. She needed to feel his warmth. This trip, they hadn't even used the sunken tub.

Parker ran his hands over her back. "I'll pour us a couple of brandies after I finish in here."

"Maybe."

She let him go, dried her hair with the towel, and pulled on a night shirt. She was just performing the ritual of tossing the pretty pillows onto the chaise lounge chair when he came out.

"I don't want any brandy," she told him.

"All right."

They climbed into bed. Before she turned off the light, she reached for her phone.

Now she felt even worse. There was a call.

Under the sheets, Parker felt her tense. "What is it?"

"It's a call from Kadera. I missed it. I turned the ringer down at the Art Institute."

He sat up. "Call him back."

She nodded.

Her fingers were trembling, but she managed to dial and put the phone on speaker.

The detective answered after two rings. "Kadera here."

"Kadera, it's Steele. You called me."

"Just about ten minutes ago."

Ten minutes? She'd assumed he'd called earlier.

"Is Mr. Parker there?"

"Yes, he's with me. I've got you on speaker."

"Good evening, Detective Kadera," Parker said in his formal way.

"Good evening, Mr. Parker. I called to let you know there's no match on the print on the plastic container you brought into the station."

What?

Miranda felt as if the mattress they were on had fallen through the floor. "What do you mean there's no match?"

"Just what I said, Steele. We ran it against everyone at the party. All the prints we took when we did the interviews of all the guests. There was no match."

Miranda turned to Parker. He seemed as bewildered as she felt.

She leaned closer to the phone. "Are you saying the print on the shampoo bottle didn't match Stella's?"

"That's what I'm saying. No match to Ms. La Stella. No match to Mrs. Prescott."

Neither of them?

"What about Dwight Donahue?" Parker said.

"No match there, either. Or anyone else at the party that night. We're running it through AFIS now. No hits yet."

The news took her breath. Miranda ran her hand through her hair wondering what to do next.

There was nothing they could do.

She stared down at the phone and realized she was still connected. "Okay. Thanks, Kadera," she said. "Let us know when you get a hit."

"Will do."

She hung up, put the phone on the nightstand, and sank down onto the mattress, feeling numb. "No matches to anyone at the party?"

Parker settled in beside her. "It seems we've been going down the wrong path."

She ran her hands over her face. "Yeah. But you know, in a weird sort of way, it makes sense. If Stella had wanted to get away with killing Prescott, she wouldn't have done it this way. She would have blamed it on Jane when she had the opportunity. She wouldn't have been upset when Jane confessed."

"That was odd on her part."

Miranda thought of standing with Parker on the terrace of the Royal Rose Hotel that afternoon. "And she wouldn't have tied Prescott's tie to the banister. She wouldn't try to make some kind of statement or bother with subtleties. When he accused her of stalking him, she would have acted on impulse. She would have pushed him over."

"The way she ran when she realized she was a suspect does show a rash nature."

Miranda stared up at the ceiling and let out a breath. "Who killed Prescott, then?"

"Perhaps one of his clients had a grudge."

Someone they hadn't even considered. "We could go back to Sikora and Vogel and follow up on that."

Parker rolled over on his side, took her chin in his hand, and turned her toward him. "Whatever the truth is, the police will discover it. It's time for us to go home, Miranda."

She blinked at him. "Home?"

"We've done all we can. We were supposed to be consultants not primary investigators." He sounded so weary.

"But—"

"It's over," he said. Then he pulled her close and kissed her hard.

She relished the taste of him. Wished she could stay under his spell forever. But she couldn't stop thinking about the case. She pulled away. "We didn't get a confession."

"Sometimes you don't. You know that." He laid back down.

She settled in beside him, leaned her head against his shoulder, and sighed.

He stroked her hair. "The police will find the match to that fingerprint, and the justice system will handle the rest. We've done our part."

She smoothed the dark hair on his chest. "What about Jane?"

"The case against her is weak. Even weaker now. I don't think they'll hold her much longer." He kissed her again and turned off the light.

"I hope not."

Miranda couldn't stand the thought of her old friend being locked up. Her kids must be asking for her. And they'd just lost their father.

But Parker was right. Going to Prescott's law firm again would be a waste of time. The fingerprint on that bottle was the key. And the police were taking care of that. There wasn't anything else they could do.

With a deep sense of defeat, she closed her eyes and went to sleep.

CHAPTER FIFTY-ONE

It was raining. Hard. It was so dark.
She sped along the highway in the red Jaguar, trying to see through the sheets of water flowing down the windshield. Sheets so heavy even the wipers couldn't clear them away.
The wipers' quick steady rhythm matched the pounding of her heart. She couldn't catch her breath.
Someone was after her. Coming up behind her. Getting closer.
Closer.
She couldn't go fast enough. She couldn't get away.
She swerved around a car on her right. The driver blared his horn at her. The maneuver hadn't helped. He was still right behind her.
She heard the roar of his engine. He was coming. She braced herself as he rammed her from behind. Her head bobbed forward and hit the windshield.
She started to bleed.
He rammed her again and her head jerked back.
She had to get away from him before he killed her.
Jamming her foot down on the accelerator as hard as she could, she steered the powerful vehicle over the slick wet pavement.
Mistake. Hydroplane.
She couldn't keep the car in the lane. It shimmied to the left, then the right. Then it ran off the road. She hit the shoulder, flew over an embankment, and landed in a large empty field.
The sudden cease of movement had her reeling. But she couldn't stay here. He was coming for her.
She scrambled out of the car and began to run.
The grass beneath her feet was slippery. Her feet slid over it. She struggled to keep going.
She could hear him panting behind her.

And then came that low ugly growl. "You can't escape me. You'll never escape me."

He was back.

No matter how hard she tried, no matter what she did, he always came back.

Around her, the grass became high. Almost to her shoulders. She pushed it away with her arms, but it was so thick. It was over her head now. She was so tired. Her whole body ached. All she wanted was to lay down in the tall grass and sleep.

No, she thought. She couldn't stop. She had to keep going.

And then all at once the grassy field opened up and a staircase appeared before her. It was a marble staircase that went up into a cloud of fog high above.

She began to climb it.

Up she went. As far as she could go. Into the clouds. Up to the sky.

And then the stairs stopped.

She found herself standing on a wide blue glass floor that stretched in every direction. There was nothing around her but the faraway clouds.

Was this Heaven? Was she dead?

"Didn't you hear me? You can't escape."

He was still there. He had followed her even up here.

Run.

It was all she could think to do. She turned and hurried across the floor as fast as she could go.

But the glassy surface was slick, and her legs were awkward on it. She couldn't keep her footing.

Her feet slid out from under her and down she went. She began to slide. She scratched at the slippery surface with her nails, but she couldn't find anything to grasp. She couldn't stop herself.

Faster and faster her body hurtled toward the end of the floor where it met the clouds. She could almost touch them now, feel their coolness.

She slid over the edge.

Her arms flailed, beating the air, grasping for something, anything.

And then her hands found a rope dangling from somewhere up above her. She clung to it with all her might as her body spun round and round in circles. The rope began to lengthen, its silky fabric stretching with her weight.

It wouldn't hold much longer. Could she climb back up?

She looked up and saw that ugly face peering over the blue edge at her, the dark hair flowing over black eyes full of hate. They glowed at her like a demon's.

Leon.

"I have you now," he croaked. "I'll put an end to you."

There was a knife in his hand.

He leaned over and began sawing at the rope.

No.

She looked down. The ground was so far away all she could see was clouds.

She looked up again. He was still hacking at the rope. He was halfway through it. She would drop soon. Down into the clouds. Down to whatever lay below.

Down to her death.

And then the knife began to make a strange buzzing sound.

Miranda's eyes popped open and she sucked in a breath. She was shaking. Her heart was pounding in her chest.

She took another breath and ran her hand over her face. Another nightmare. Leon chasing her through some fantastic place in her imagination.

Wait.

She could still hear that buzzing sound. She glanced at the nightstand and grimaced. It was her cell phone.

Kadera?

Sitting up, she grabbed the phone and looked for the latest text.

It wasn't from Kadera. It was from Victoria Winslow. Vaguely Miranda recalled giving the woman her card with her cell number at the station.

I'm sorry to bother you at this hour. After seeing you tonight, I remembered something I need to tell you. I'm working late, doing inventory at the restaurant. Can you meet me here?

At this hour? Miranda looked at the time. Almost one in the morning. She turned and saw Parker sleeping peacefully beside her. What could Victoria Winslow have to say that would help Jane?

She thumbed a reply.

I can meet you at the police station tomorrow.

Half a minute passed.

I don't think it can wait until then.

Maybe it was important. If it was something that could get Jane off the hook and get her back home with her kids, it was worth hearing no matter what time it was.

She looked at Parker again. His handsome face wore a serene expression. She knew he was tired, especially tired of this case. He'd made it clear he wanted to go home. If Victoria gave them another lead that would extend the case, he wouldn't be happy.

She didn't want to fight with him about it.

She could handle this by herself. She didn't need to disturb him.

The Sapphire Grille? She thumbed back.

Yes.

I'll be there in fifteen minutes. It was just across the river and down the street.

Quietly she slipped out of bed, found some jeans, pulled on a long sleeved shirt, and put on her running shoes. As she grabbed her wallet, she decided to take the Glock Templeton had loaned her. She assumed Parker had intended to return the weapons tomorrow.

She probably wouldn't need it, but just in case, she slipped the holster over her shoulder, threw on a jacket and went into the living room of the suite.

Better leave a note.

She found paper and pen in a side desk and began to scribble.

Got a text from Winslow. She has something to tell me. Meeting her at The Sapphire Grille at one. Yes, in the morning. Be back soon.

With any luck she could crumble up the note and crawl back into bed with him in half an hour.

Or she could wake him up, and they could call Templeton with news that would free Jane.

Hoping for the best, she went down to the lobby of the hotel and caught a taxi.

CHAPTER FIFTY-TWO

It was about ten past one when the cab pulled up to the curb on North Wacker.

Miranda stared out at the tall deserted skyscrapers and caught sight of The Sapphire Grille's windows and its shiny sign on the ground floor of one of them.

The restaurant was as dark as the rest of the street.

She handed the driver some bills. "Wait for me. I won't be long."

"I can't wait long, lady."

Ignoring him, she got out of the cab and hurried to the restaurant's entrance.

Inside, the lights were off. The "We're Closed" sign hung silently in the window. The staff must be in the back, doing inventory as Victoria had said.

Miranda banged on the door, hoping the woman could hear her.

No answer.

She cupped her hands against the pane and peered inside. Rows and rows of chairs were stacked atop rows and rows of tables. Low night lights cast long shadows on the polished floor. She didn't see anyone in the dining area. Along the far back wall stood an open entryway to the kitchen. No movement there. No signs of life at all.

She knocked on the door again and waited.

Nothing.

Shoving her hands in her pockets, she stepped back and looked around.

Feeling antsy, she eyed the narrow road between the building housing the restaurant and the neighboring skyscraper. Maybe there was a back way in.

She jogged over to the cabbie. "I'm going to check down there. I'll only be a minute."

He shook his head. "Lady, I can't wait much longer."

"Five minutes."

"If I get another call, I gotta go."

"Just wait for me."

She jogged over to the corner.

A bistro with an outdoor dining area occupied the corner on the other side of the road. Its chairs were stacked on its tables, and it sported a "Closed" sign, too. Everything looked deserted. Silent planters lined the walkway along the bistro's edge.

Miranda stepped off the sidewalk and onto the pavement. Pausing a moment, she pulled out her Glock. Not too smart to roam the alleys of a big city at night without a weapon in your hand.

Cautiously she began making her way between the buildings.

Along the near side of the alley stretched three large side windows belonging to The Sapphire Grille. The last one had the shades drawn. Was that the kitchen?

She ran over to it and knocked on the glass.

Nothing.

She turned around and gazed at the wall beyond the bistro. A vented metal housing for utilities covered the building and seemed to rise up to the sky.

The Grille's building ran down the alley about another twenty feet. Beyond that, the wall turned to brick, ascending nearly as high as its neighbor.

There was a space between the back of the building housing the Grille and the rear of the skyscraper on the next block.

It was another alley, perpendicular to the one she stood in, forming a T shape.

She moved to it and stared down the passageway. It was really dark down there, but she could make out a back door. It had to belong to the Grille.

Slipping her gun into its holster for a moment, she took out her phone and thumbed a message to Victoria.

Where are you?

She waited. No answer there, either.

She heard an engine growl, turned her head and saw the cab drive away.

You jerk.

Taking a deep breath, she pulled out her Glock again, stepped into the darkness, and headed for the door.

Reaching it, she studied the metal frame in the illumination from a small light mounted on the wall.

Its dark paint was scratched and dented. It had seen better days. The smell of old food and grease came from somewhere.

And then that strange familiar sensation crept up the back of her neck, making her skin prickle and her stomach tense.

She ignored it.

Might as well see if this was the back entrance. Maybe it was noisy inside and Victoria hadn't heard her knocking at the front. Or her cell buzz.

She banged on the door with her fist. "Victoria? You said you had something to tell me. I'm here."

No answer.

She tried the handle.

Locked.

This was crazy. Nobody was in there doing inventory. She never should have come here. Now she'd have to get another cab.

What could Victoria Winslow tell her that she didn't already know anyway? Certainly she didn't know anything about that partial print on that vial. It didn't even match anyone at the party.

Suddenly Miranda remembered Victoria had said she'd left the party early. She hadn't been questioned by the police that night.

They hadn't taken her fingerprints.

Then she felt something hard against the back of her head. And heard that refined, soft spoken voice.

"I'm here, too, Miranda. Drop the gun."

CHAPTER FIFTY-THREE

Parker rolled over in bed and reached for his wife. He was half asleep, but he could tell she wasn't there.

Groggily he forced his eyes open and squinted into the shadows. No light under the bathroom door.

"Miranda?" he called.

There was no answer.

Concerned, he pulled back the covers and sat up.

"Miranda."

Did she have another nightmare and decide to sleep on the couch?

He rose and went to the living room to check. He turned on the light and scanned the room. She wasn't here.

A hard knot began to form in his gut.

For an instant, his mind went back to those long painful days when he'd thought she was dead. Once more, he saw her running toward him on that inky fish pier in Boston. Once more, he heard the crack of gunfire and saw her body jerk back as the bullet hit her. Once more, he saw her go down on the pavement.

Where in the world was she?

And then he noticed a piece of paper on the desk. He hurried over to it and picked it up.

She'd left him a note. She hadn't wanted to wake him with a text.

Anger burned inside him. This was a reversion to what things had been like between them when they were first married. During their first cases together. Worse. How could she go out on her own in the middle of the night after what they'd just been through?

He read the note quickly. Sapphire Grille. Victoria Winslow.

His mind went back to that woman's interview and the things she had said about Stella. Stella had denied most of it. But she had also lied about the oxycodone. She had tried to run from the police. She wasn't trustworthy.

And then he thought of the fingerprint the police were trying to match. All at once the pieces clicked into place.

Dear Lord.

He glanced at the note again. She'd left at one in the morning, it said. He eyed the digital clock on the desk.

It was almost one-thirty.

He hurried back to the bedroom, threw on casual clothes, dark ones, and his black running shoes. He reached into the drawer for the Glock from the police station and saw Miranda had taken hers.

That gave him some hope. But not enough.

Strapping on the shoulder holster, several worse case scenarios went through his mind. He slipped the Glock into the holster, reached for his black leather jacket from the closet, and hurried out the door.

He only hoped the Jaguar would start. If it didn't and he couldn't get a cab, he would run all the way there.

CHAPTER FIFTY-FOUR

Miranda turned around, put her free hand on her hip, and stared straight into the barrel of a Sig Sauer compact. A weapon made for small hands.

"Hello, Victoria. Is that part of your inventory?"

Anger flashed across the woman's face. "I said, put down your gun."

Miranda raised her hands, but kept the weapon. "Is that what you forgot to tell me? That you have a gun? Is that thing registered?"

"Of course it is. And I know how to use it, too."

She sounded like Stella. It was too risky not to believe her. Still, Miranda hesitated, waiting for an opportunity to turn the tables.

"Are you going to make me shoot you right here, Miranda?" Victoria grunted.

"Where did you plan to shoot me?"

"Put the gun down. Now." Victoria's voice wasn't soft anymore. She sounded hysterical.

Miranda didn't like her choices, but if she waited much longer, Victoria might pull the trigger. She decided if she could keep the woman talking, she might let down her guard and she could get that Sig away from her.

Slowly she bent her knees and laid her Glock down on the pavement.

As soon as she had straightened again, Victoria kicked the gun over to a stack of plastic crates along the wall. It clattered against the bricks.

Miranda scowled at her. "You know that's police property, don't you?"

"So?"

"They might not appreciate your treating their equipment that way."

"I don't care what the police think."

"That's pretty apparent." And to think, just a couple days ago, Miranda had thought Victoria had come to the station out of a sense of civic duty.

Miranda studied the woman's oblong face, longish nose, and narrow chin. She was feeling bold tonight and didn't have it tucked into her neck in that shy way of hers.

Then she noticed a notch on that chin. A scar.

Miranda remembered her flashback at the Art Institute that evening. It was Victoria Stella had tripped on the stairs.

Now it made sense. This thing went way back, didn't it?

"You were in love with Quinton Prescott since high school, weren't you?"

Victoria's mouth opened in shock.

"He rejected you, didn't he? He chose Stella over you."

Victoria gave her a vicious grimace. "He didn't reject me. He saw me behind Stella's back. He made love to me."

Now it was Miranda's turn to be shocked. "He what?"

"He made love to me," Victoria said as if she thought Miranda was an idiot. "He told me I was his whole world. I was everything he ever wanted. His one and only."

Like he had said to so many other women. Wow. Prescott was two-timing Stella with the likes of Victoria Winslow? He had really gotten an early start at the cheating game.

Victoria jabbed her gun in Miranda's side. "Get moving. That way." She nodded toward the open end of the side alley.

"Where are we going?"

"You'll find out when we get there."

Miranda studied the gun in Victoria's hand. If only she knew how quick the woman's reflexes were.

"I said move." Victoria jabbed her in the ribs again.

It hurt this time.

"Okay, okay."

Miranda turned and slowly started toward the other alley, moving farther and farther away from her Glock.

CHAPTER FIFTY-FIVE

Keep her talking, Miranda told herself as they plodded over the pavement. "If you were Prescott's one and only, why didn't you two end up together after high school?"

"It wasn't because of Stella." Victoria walked a little behind her, keeping the gun in her ribs.

Miranda moved as slowly as she dared. "No?"

She sneered. "Quinton told me he'd never marry her. She wasn't the right type of wife for the career he had planned. He broke up with her right after graduation. I waited for him to propose to me instead. I called him and called him. He didn't answer. Then he changed his number."

He was dumping both of them, like he always did. Maybe sympathy would get to her. "You must have been brokenhearted. What did you do?"

"I got a job and tried to forget him. But I followed his career and his life. I saw the wedding announcement in the paper when he married Jane Anderson. And the birth announcements when he had his two sons. I knew he was working at Sikora and Vogel. I saw the announcement when he made partner."

She hadn't forgotten him at all.

And then one evening, she saw him having dinner with Stella at The Sapphire Grille. She'd probably seen him with other women before that, but the idea of Prescott with Stella together after all this time must have driven her crazy.

They reached the intersection of the alleys and Victoria turned her away from the restaurants.

"This way."

They started down the dark passage.

A chilly wind blew through the alley, yet Miranda could feel the sweat drops forming along her hairline.

She scanned the brick wall of the next building. Conduit for wire and cabling ran along the length of it. Nothing there she could use as a weapon.

They passed the loading docks where she had seen delivery trucks the day she and Parker and Templeton ate at The Sapphire Grille.

And then Miranda remembered something.

In her interview at the police station, Victoria had pretended not to even know Stella's name. She said she'd left Stella and Prescott standing together at the banister of the rooftop terrace.

She'd lied.

Miranda came to a sudden halt. "Where did you get the oxycodone?"

"What? I—I don't know what you're talking about," Victoria sputtered, startled by the question.

"A high level of oxycodone was found in Prescott's blood."

Suddenly Victoria's demeanor changed as if she were turning into a different person. She glared at Miranda, then she lifted her head almost gloating with pride. "I got it from Quinton's medicine cabinet."

Medicine cabinet? Where Miranda had found it? "How did you get into his house?"

Surely Prescott hadn't invited this woman there.

Victoria's expression grew even more smug. "I volunteered to help Jane with the reunion party committee. I only went to his house twice. It was enough. I found that bottle in the master bath and took five tablets from it. I was going to use a couple of tablets to make him groggy enough to sign divorce papers, and then use a few more later to get him to a judge and marry me, but it didn't work out that way."

"You couldn't get him alone long enough?"

She seemed surprised at the question. "We were alone a lot."

They were? "When?"

"He noticed me at the Grille. He was by himself one night, and I sat down at his table. We started to talk. We exchanged numbers, but we never texted. He called me when he wanted to be together. It was right after Christmas that we started seeing each other several times a week. We went to different hotels around the city. Nice ones. We made love over and over."

Christmas. That was after Prescott had told Jane he wanted to mend their marriage. So much for that idea.

"And then Quinton told me he was getting back with his wife. I told him I was the one who was meant to be his wife. I kept calling him, waiting for him to come to his senses. I would follow him when he went out of the office. And then I thought, the reunion party was my chance. He'd remember how it was between us in high school. That night I tried to talk to him, but he avoided me. Then I saw him on the terrace at the banister. I went up to him and told him we were meant to be together. I told him I was the only one for him. But he wouldn't listen to me. He told me to get away from him."

She was the "woman trouble" Prescott told Donahue about.

Miranda thought of what Victoria had said at the police station and turned to face her. "Prescott didn't tell Stella to stop stalking him the night of the reunion party. That's what he said to you, wasn't it?"

Suddenly Victoria's eyes began to tear up. "I don't know why he said that to me. I loved him so much. No one could love him like I did. No one else deserved him."

That part was probably true. "And so you put the oxycodone pills in his drink."

"I ground them up right after I took them. I kept them in my pocket in a TSA shampoo bottle. I carried it with me all the time. Waiting for a chance."

The bottle she and Parker had found in the stairwell. The one they had taken to the police. The one with the partial fingerprint that belonged to Victoria.

She must have heard them talking about it at the Willis Tower tonight. That was why she'd sent her that text. That was why Miranda was standing with her in a dark alley now, with her gun pointed at her.

But now, everything was spilling out of the woman.

"Right after Stella left," Victoria sniffed, "I slipped the powder into a dry martini. I went over and handed Quinton the drink. He swallowed it down without even a second thought. I was so angry with him. I was going to push him over that banister. He would have been too intoxicated to even notice. And then I thought no, that was too good for him. I decided he should be hanged."

Miranda thought of what Stella had said about Prescott's tie. "You saw Stella grab his tie earlier, didn't you? You did that to pin his murder on her."

"Why not? She was always such a stuck up bitch. She had everything. Looks. Pretty clothes. All the boys in school wanted her. She could have had any one of them. Why did she have to take mine?"

This woman was so deluded, Miranda almost felt sorry for her. But she had to get the rest of what happened out of her.

"So you tied the end of Prescott's tie to the banister, gave him a push, and he toppled right over." Victoria had been wearing dress gloves with her gown that night. That's why her prints weren't on the tie along with Stella's.

"I stood watching him for a while. His face turned blue. He kicked and grabbed at his tie, trying to get loose. He saw me and stretched out his hand to me, begging for help."

Miranda's stomach churned at the image. "And?"

"And that's when I ran. I was in a panic. I couldn't pull him back over the banister, and I wasn't sure I wanted to. I knew there was a side door that led to the kitchen. One of our busboys at the Grille used to work there and told me about it. I went down some stairs. That's when I pulled off my gloves and put them in my pocket. I found the shampoo bottle in there and tossed it in a corner. I thought one of the workers would find it and throw it away. And then I went out through the kitchen."

The bottle must have picked up the print then, or maybe from when she'd carried it around.

Miranda realized something else. "You never saw Stella in the bathroom."

"No."

"How did you know she'd go there?"

"Lucky guess. She'd been crying. She was supposed to be with Jane at the podium. I figured she'd want to clean herself up first."

Miranda owed Stella an apology. If she could stay alive long enough to see her again.

Victoria wiped her face with the back of her hand and steadied her Sig. "Now that you know everything, you can see why I have to get rid of you. My car's in a parking garage down the street. We're going to go there. We'll get in, and you'll drive to where I tell you."

Some secluded forest preserve, she imagined.

"If we see anyone and you try to call for help, I'll shoot you and them, too."

She knew Miranda might sacrifice herself, but not innocent bystanders. Victoria wouldn't be able to get rid of all the bodies, but she probably wouldn't care at that point.

"So once more, get moving." She jabbed her again with the gun.

CHAPTER FIFTY-SIX

Miranda scowled down at the Sig in her ribs, then turned and began to walk again.

She eyed the brick walls of the alley. There had to be a way out. Something. Anything. But right now, she couldn't see it.

She peered down the passage to where the highway crossed it. No cars passed by. This was a business district. The streets that had been so crowded with traffic and pedestrians during the day were deserted at this hour.

There wouldn't be any help there.

She had to get the gun away from this maniac before they got to the sidewalk.

Maybe she could rattle her. "Victoria, your fingerprint is on that bottle you tossed away."

"I know. I heard you talking about it with your husband at the Willis Building."

She knew it. "Once the police match it, they'll know you killed Prescott. You don't want a second murder charge, do you?"

She laughed, her refined voice echoing up between the buildings. "I'm not worried about that. They won't find your body. Once you're dead, I'll toss you in the Chicago River, or maybe I'll drive up to the northern part of Lake Michigan and drop you in a secluded place up there. And then I'll leave the country. I'm tired of Chicago. There are too many memories of Quinton here."

There was no changing her mind. She was in her own world where she made up the rules. And even though she claimed to love Prescott and had sniffled a little, she hadn't broken down and bawled.

She was cold.

Miranda would have to find another way to distract her.

They walked along, the only sounds around them their footsteps on the asphalt. Then she heard the sudden whoosh of a lone car on the street passing the alley.

That was it.

Miranda turned her head and peered down the alley. "Look." She pointed toward the main road. "Isn't that a police car? I think it's stopping."

It worked. Panic on her face, Victoria turned her gaze toward the opening for just a second.

Long enough.

Quickly Miranda brought her leg up and spun around in a high kick. Her foot hit Victoria square on the forearm, knocking the gun out of her hand.

Twisting and stumbling, Victoria let out a guttural growl. Then she recovered and dove for the Sig.

Miranda hated to do it, but she had no choice. She took a step, raised her leg again, and kicked the woman in the face.

Not as hard as she could, but enough to knock her away.

With a cry of shock and pain, Victoria fell to the pavement. She rolled over onto her back groaning and holding her hands over her face. "What are you doing? Are you crazy?"

"You think *I'm* crazy?" Miranda bent down to get the gun.

"No, you don't." Victoria rose to her knees.

She shot up from the pavement and lunged at Miranda, grabbing the opening of her jacket. Somehow pulling herself to her feet, with the force of a small rhino, she spun Miranda around and hurled her toward the wall.

Miranda landed against the bricks with a thud that took her breath.

That bitch was a lot stronger than she looked. Must be the adrenaline.

Miranda had some of that, too.

She came at Victoria again, this time punching with her fists. Victoria put her arms up to block, but she was no match for a trained fighter.

Miranda landed a right on her chin, then a left on her jaw. Then another hard right that sent Victoria flying into the opposite wall.

Victoria caught herself against the bricks and screamed. "What are you doing?" She put her palms to her face and looked down at her hands. "I'm bleeding."

That was from the kick to the face. "That can happen when you get into a street fight."

They were near the spot where Miranda had seen bicycles and motorcycles parked the other day. Now the area was empty, a row of protective metal bollard poles delineating the section of the pavement.

The Sig lay about two feet away from the last rod, its metal sheen reflecting the light from the street.

Once again Miranda bent down to get it, her fingers reaching for the pistol.

She was two inches away from the handle when she heard a cry like some banshee from hell.

Victoria lunged toward her, grabbed her extended arm, and spun her around like a deranged ballerina.

She let go and again Miranda went flying. But this time she was heading toward the thick metal poles.

Fear sliced through her. Out of control.

She put out her hands, but she couldn't stop herself. Miranda saw the parking pole coming toward her. She tried to turn away, but it didn't work.

Her head connected with the hard metal.

She heard a crunch. She hit the pavement. The alley began to spin.

And then there was nothing. Nothing.

Nothing but darkness all around her. An empty vacuum. So devoid of life, even Leon wouldn't come here.

And then she heard a strange echoing sound. A voice.

She was coming to. Her head ached, but she hadn't been out long. Or at least she didn't think so.

Miranda opened her eyes and saw a hazy figure standing over her. The figure was talking, but she wasn't making any sense.

"What?"

As her vision cleared Miranda raised her head off the asphalt. She was lying on her back, gazing up at the talking figure.

Victoria stood over her, the Sig pointed at her heart.

"I said, you leave me no choice, Miranda. I'll have to shoot you here and get my car and put you in the trunk. Or maybe I'll leave you here. The police will just think you're another mugging victim in a Chicago alley. You won't even make the news."

Victoria Winslow was definitely crazy.

But Miranda had dealt with crazy before. She had to tell her something. Anything.

She put up her hands in surrender. "Don't shoot, Victoria. I won't tell anyone what you told me tonight. I'll tell the police you gave me the shampoo bottle and I made up a story about finding it in the stairwell."

"They wouldn't believe you."

"Yes, they would. I can tell them I wanted to get even with you for cheating off of me on chemistry tests in high school."

"I never cheated. I made good grades."

"I'll tell them I had a crush on Prescott, too. I wanted to get back at you."

"Please." She didn't buy that at all.

"I'll think of something. I can make sure Stella gets convicted for Prescott's murder."

That seemed to make her stop and think a minute. But then she shook her head. "No, you won't. You're sneaky. You can't be trusted."

She raised the gun.

"No. Wait."

"I can't wait any longer. Goodbye, my dear high school friend."

Her heart hammering in her chest, desperately Miranda tried to crawl away on her elbows. This couldn't be happening. After surviving Santana's bullet in Boston, was she going to be killed by this demon possessed shrew?

No. No.

But Victoria stepped closer.

She shivered with fear. Her ears pounded with it.

Victoria steadied the gun, about to squeeze the trigger.

Miranda braced herself for the shot.

Think. If she could maneuver her body the right way, maybe it wouldn't hit a vital organ. Or an artery. She just had to be fast enough.

But she had taken too long to think about it. before Miranda could move, she heard the blast.

She closed her eyes and waited for the jolt of pain.

She didn't feel anything.

Instead she opened her eyes again and watched Victoria's face go blank. Still hovering over her, the woman tottered one way, then the other. She stumbled forward, then back. Then the gun fell out of her hand and she crumbled to the ground.

Stunned Miranda stared at her. Then behind her, she heard running.

She turned her head and saw Parker coming toward her, his police weapon drawn.

He'd shot her. He'd shot Victoria Winslow and saved her life. Again.

The next instant he was kneeling beside her, cradling her in his arms. "Oh, my darling, my darling. Are you hurt? Are you injured?"

"No. I'm fine." Except for her aching head and being scared out of her wits. She thought about that note she'd left him. "I'm sorry I went out alone. It was stupid. I should have woken you up."

"Never mind that." He touched her face and gazed at her as if it was the first time he'd seen her. "Oh, my love. I'm just so glad you're alive."

And he pulled her close and smothered her with kisses.

CHAPTER FIFTY-SEVEN

Miranda hadn't been that far off about the police.

The instant Parker reached her, squad car lights flashed and sirens screamed on the adjacent street. She heard more running footsteps.

They turned out to be Kadera and his uniformed compadres—just in time to see Parker nail their killer.

"What a coincidence," Kadera smirked as he took in the scene. "Victoria Winslow's name popped as the match to that fingerprint right after Mr. Parker called."

Parker called the police?

And the fingerprint on that shampoo bottle was Victoria's. Well, that's what she'd admitted to her. Miranda was glad there was proof now.

"Thanks for responding," Miranda told Kadera as Parker helped her up.

"No problem. You'll be glad to know Mrs. Prescott is being released as we speak."

Thank God.

With Parker's steadying arm around her, Miranda watched the officers go over to the body and examine the scene while Kadera stepped away to take a call on his cell.

The sight of Victoria's lifeless body made her dizzy.

Miranda put a hand to her aching head.

"Are you all right? Do you need a doctor?" Parker would take her to the hospital right now if she let him.

"I'm okay. Just a bump on the noggin. I wasn't out that long." She'd have a big knot by morning.

Gently he kissed her cheek, right in front of the officers, though they weren't paying much attention. "We'll make an appointment with Jackson when we get home."

"Okay." She'd let him baby her. Right now, it felt good.

"Can you handle things here, Enzo?" she heard Kadera say to one of the men.

"Absolutely, sir."

Kadera pointed to her and Parker. "I'll take statements from these two. First, I want to show them something."

"What do you have to show us, Detective?" Parker wanted to know.

"You'll have to see it to believe it."

In a daze, Miranda followed Kadera to a Tahoe similar to Templeton's. She climbed into the backseat with Parker and stared at the police car lights as they rolled away.

They rode down the Eisenhower and out to the suburbs. Less than half an hour later, Kadera pulled over to the curb near a narrow blue house in Berwyn.

Another squad car with its lights flashing sat in front of the house. Neighbors were out in their pajamas and coats. An officer stood on the porch talking to an elderly couple Miranda assumed were the owners.

"This is the address Winslow gave when she came in to give her statement the other night. I sent Bradley over here as soon as her name popped."

As if he'd heard Kadera talking about him, the officer on the porch jogged over to the Tahoe.

"Owners have given you permission to enter, sir," he told Kadera. "There's a second entry around the back."

Sounded like he'd already been inside.

They got out of the Tahoe and headed toward the rear.

As they made their way through the narrow space between the houses, Kadera filled them in. "We learned Winslow was fired from a South Loop elementary school this past February. Her mother passed away a year ago and her performance degraded after that. After she was fired, Winslow went a little nuts and was arrested for disorderly conduct."

"So she didn't take the job at The Sapphire Grille to pay for her mother's medical expenses," Miranda said.

"No, looks like she had another reason for that."

Officer Bradley led them over to the back door, which was open. They climbed up four wooden steps and entered a small dingy living room filled with what looked like second hand furniture.

Other than needing a good cleaning, there was nothing special about it.

"The kicker is back there." Bradley pointed across the room.

Kadera led them down a short hall and into the bedroom. When he looked around, he let out a low whistle.

Miranda wanted to do the same.

"Good Lord," Parker murmured beside her.

There was a small single bed in the corner, neatly made with a dark coverlet. The floor was dark, and the walls were painted black.

But you could hardly tell that for the photos. There must have been over a hundred of them covering every surface.

Every one was of Prescott.

Prescott in high school. Prescott in his football uniform leading the team to a touchdown. Prescott in a suit at the school council meeting wearing his infamous tie. Homecoming photos of Prescott and Stella. Prom photos of Prescott and Stella. A copy of the photo they'd found in Stella's desk at the TV station. Then there were lots of photos of Prescott from college. And at work at Sikora and Vogel. She must have gotten those off the law firm's website.

And there were more personal ones—pictures Victoria must have taken with her phone.

Prescott exiting the train at Union Station. Prescott getting out of his car in a parking garage. Prescott stepping into the elevator of his office building. Prescott dining with various women at The Sapphire Grille. Stella was in several shots. Her face was scratched out in some of them, but it was her.

Miranda drew in a breath. "She *was* stalking him."

"There's no kinder way to say it," Parker agreed.

Kadera turned to them with a contrite expression. "Thanks for being so persistent on this one. Otherwise we would have really gotten it wrong."

Miranda nodded, but she had no words.

Kadera took them back to the crime scene and took their statements, then they drove back to the hotel in the beat up Jaguar.

As she climbed into bed next to Parker, all Miranda could do was hug him close. He did the same.

They fell asleep holding each other in a tight embrace.

CHAPTER FIFTY-EIGHT

Neither of them felt like eating the next day, but Parker insisted on a light breakfast of scrambled eggs and toast in the hotel restaurant.

Then they packed their bags and left.

It was out of the way, but Miranda wanted to stop by and see Jane before they said goodbye to everyone at the police station. As Kadera had said, Jane had been released last night and had spent the night in her house.

Miranda sat on the sofa next to Parker in Jane's cozy blue den sipping coffee, while Jane tried to take in the events of last night as Miranda related them to her friend..

Jane stared off into space. "I can't believe it was Victoria Winslow. She was always such a shy, quiet girl."

"Still waters run deep," Parker said, setting down his cup.

Deep and dark in this case.

"We used to do homework together in the library. She was at the house to work on the reunion party."

"That's when she took the oxycodone pills," Miranda told her. She thought Jane had a right to know that.

Jane nodded solemnly as she studied her coffee. "The police let me talk to Stella before I left the station. They're charging her with aggravated fleeing and resisting arrest because of the high speed chase she led them on, but of course, they've dropped the murder charge. Her lawyer told me he thinks she'll be out in about thirty days. Maybe less."

Miranda felt a twinge of guilt. "Tell her I'm sorry I suspected her."

"She understands. All the evidence pointed to her. She wanted me to thank you both for finding the real killer."

That made Miranda smile. "No problem."

Jane put down her cup and sat back in her chair. "And now I'm back to putting the pieces of my life back together. I guess I'm better off without Quinton."

Miranda didn't say anything. She agreed, but she wasn't going to say it out loud. Jane had been through too much.

"Oh, I forgot to tell you. When I got my cell back there was a message from a New York editor."

"Really?"

"She wants to turn my mommy blog into a book."

A New York editor wanted to publish the mommy blog? Miranda was surprised. "That's great."

"She's going to call next week and we'll start working on the details. I'm excited about it."

Miranda didn't know how that had happened, but it was a new direction for Jane's life and she was happy for her friend.

They chatted for a few more minutes, then Parker rose. "Thank you for the coffee, Jane. We'd better be on our way."

With a nod, Jane got to her feet. "So you're heading back to Atlanta right away?"

"That's the plan."

At the door, Jane opened it and leaned against the frame as she gazed out at the yard. "I think I'll take the boys to Europe myself this summer."

"That would be nice," Miranda told her, glad she was trying to make happy memories for them.

"Mother will be bringing them home this afternoon after school. I can't wait to see them and give them both a big hug."

Another happy memory, though it would be bittersweet. But they had each other. Time would pass. The family would heal.

"Will Stella still have her forecaster job after she gets out?"

"I think so. The meteorologist is going to bat for her at the station. I think he's going to ask her out when she's released."

Same old Stella La Stella.

Jane shook Parker's hand and gave Miranda a big hug. "We'll have to keep in touch."

"That would be nice."

"Have a safe trip home."

"Thank you, Jane."

"Thank you. Both of you."

And they left her on the doorstep and headed for the Jag.

CHAPTER FIFTY-NINE

When they walked into the cube bank at the Larrabee station, Miranda and Parker were greeted with hoots and applause.

Demarco came around the corner from his office and hurried over to shake their hands. "You two are heroes around here."

"All in a day's work," Parker said, taking the sergeant's hand. "Or should I say evening's?"

Demarco chuckled. "Glad you're a twenty-four-seven kind of operation."

Miranda had to grimace at that one.

"Say, I'm just about to give an official press conference out front. Would you like to join me?"

Parker turned to Miranda.

He wanted her to make the call? That was an easy one. "If you don't mind, Demarco, we'll sit this one out."

The toothpick in his mouth switched sides as he laughed. "Can't say that I blame you. You're heading back home?"

"We have a flight in a few hours," Parker said, satisfaction in his voice.

"Well, thanks again. Anytime you're in town feel free to stop by."

"Thanks." But Miranda didn't think that would be happening anytime soon.

"I'd better get out there. Take care, you two." As he turned to hurry down the passage, he called out, "Templeton, ten minutes."

"Yes, sir." Templeton's curly head popped up from a cube. Then she came around to shake hands as well.

"Where have you been?" Miranda asked.

"Working another case." She took both of their hands. "Thank you both for saving my butt on this one. Without you, we would have put away two innocent people."

"You were just doing your job," Parker told her.

She let his hand go and gave each of them a meaningful look. "Speaking of which, can I show you something?"

"Sure." They had a plane to catch, but they could spare a few minutes.

Templeton led them back around the cubes to her desk. There were papers strewn across it, some of them were photos that looked pretty grisly.

This must be the case Templeton had been pulled to work. That meant Demarco was trusting her with more responsibility.

She picked up one of the photos. "The vic was female. Just twenty years old. Found in Hyde Park early yesterday."

Miranda looked down at the picture and her stomach turned. Long blond hair spread out on the dirty damp ground. The naked body pale and covered with knife wounds.

"Looks like we've got a slasher on our hands."

"I'll say."

"Are you sure you two wouldn't want to stay on and help with this case?"

Help Templeton find another killer? This one a lot more vicious.

Miranda turned to Parker.

His face was expressionless. Purposely, she knew. He wanted her to decide.

She looked down at the photo and felt the calling in her heart. The need to right wrongs. Her destiny. It had been the purpose they'd shared once.

Then she remembered the image of Parker being shot down on a dark fish pier in Boston. And the sting of a bullet going through her shoulder. And what she'd put him through last night.

She shook her head. "Sorry, Templeton. Maybe another time."

CHAPTER SIXTY

"What are the car rental folks going to say about the state of the Jag?"

They were cruising down the Kennedy Expressway, on their way to O'Hare International to catch the next flight back to Atlanta. At last.

Parker surged ahead of a smelly tank truck and got in front of it. "I'll tell them I have insurance."

"Will it cover everything?"

"I'll offer to pay for whatever it doesn't."

Which could be a pretty penny, but Parker never worried about money.

A taxi veered into their lane and Parker slowed. "What was the text you got when we left the station?"

They'd snuck out the back and had somehow avoided being snagged by reporters this time. While they were crossing the parking lot, her phone had buzzed.

"It was from Mackenzie. She's on school break and traveling in Scotland with her parents."

"That sounds nice."

"Yeah." She missed her daughter, but that wasn't what was bothering her right now. She stared out at the traffic and the billboards and thought about that photograph of the dead young woman.

Finally she had to say it. "Did we do the right thing about Templeton's new case, Parker?"

Parker's chest expanded as he inhaled. He changed lanes again before answering in a low intense tone. "Do you want to come out of retirement, Miranda?"

She wasn't expecting that question. "We haven't done so well with it so far, have we?"

"Your high school reunion was not what I imagined it would be."

He didn't sound angry. Just resigned to how things had turned out.

It had been her idea to retire. She'd thought they'd faced enough vicious killers. She'd thought they'd risk their lives enough times. Templeton was a good detective. Kadera wasn't bad, either, and they had a whole team of cops behind them. They could handle that case.

She sat up straight. "No, I don't want to give up on retirement. We slipped up this time. We'll just have to go home and try harder." And find something meaningful to do with their lives.

A slow easy smile spread over Parker's face.

Just then her cell phone dinged.

She dug it out of her pocket and looked at the screen. "Uh oh."

"What is it?"

"I got a text from Gen."

"Oh?"

She held the phone up and read. "*We have baby showers to plan. Coco and Fanuzzi are due soon.*" She sunk down in the bucket seat with a groan.

Parker chuckled.

Miranda rolled her eyes. "Dealing with that slasher might be easier than planning baby showers with Gen."

Before Parker could answer, his cell buzzed.

Since he was driving, he handed the phone to her.

She took it and read the message. "It's Holloway. He wants to meet with you."

"Regarding what?"

"He doesn't say. Probably thought I would read his text."

Parker was silent a moment as he took the fork on the expressway that led to the airport. "I haven't sublet the penthouse yet. How do you feel about staying there a few days instead of heading back to the cabin?"

"You want to go back to the penthouse?"

"You have baby showers to plan and Holloway wants to meet with us about something."

Us. He wasn't going to let Holloway leave her out.

Sitting back, she thought about Parker's suggestion. Yeah, she'd like to go back to the penthouse for a while. "I'm good with that plan. Maybe we can find a place to take dancing lessons."

"That sounds delightful." With a smile on his face, he squeezed her hand.

"Yeah, it does." She leaned over and kissed his cheek.

All he wanted was for her to be safe. She wanted the same for him.

They had made it out of this one alive, but it had been close. Surely they could make a go of retirement. They had a lifetime of love to look forward to, even if she did have to deal with Gen every once in a while.

She gazed into the side mirror. The sky was a bright blue and the city buildings had disappeared behind them. She thought back on that dark alley where she'd nearly died last night.

Whatever was in store for them, she'd make sure she'd never take a risk like that again.

CHAPTER SIXTY-ONE

He sat cross-legged on his bed, munching corn chips from a bag and letting the crumbs drop onto the dirty spread as he watched the television on the dresser.

When her face came on the screen, a whole chip fell out of his mouth and onto the bed.

It was her. Impossible.

But there she was. Miranda Steele. With her thick dark hair and intense blue eyes. She was telling the reporter how good the police were. Hah.

But the footage of her was taken at night. It was daytime now. The image on the screen switched to a man in a light blue business shirt and tie standing outside a police station.

He listened carefully.

The man spoke about a recent case. The murder of a local attorney. The news people had been covering the story since Sunday. He had been busy. He hadn't been watching much TV.

The man told the reporters the case was closed. Closed. That meant she'd left town, right?

Went back to Atlanta with that rich husband of hers. Right?

The story ended and a commercial came on. Silly music played as colorful sponges danced across the screen.

He switched off the TV with the remote, shoved the chip bag onto the nightstand, and went to his computer.

He found the news story online, ran the video from the other night until her face appeared again. He hit the pause button, then print.

Patiently he waited as his printer rumbled to life and churned out the page.

He picked up the paper and studied the distinctive features. He ran his hand over her cheek. There was both hardness and gentleness in her eyes.

He longed to see them look into his as he turned their expression into sheer terror.

Rising he found a thumb tack on his desk and searched for a spot on the wall. There were others there. His collection. His past and future projects.

There were already several photos of Miranda Steele.

He put her in the middle of the others so that she'd be the first he would see when he woke in the morning.

He had other projects to finish first, but he would get her. He would travel wherever he needed to.

After all, that's what his dead mentor had done. He had failed before, but he wouldn't fail this time.

Once more he touched her cheek and felt a surge of excitement rise up from his groin. He would get her. He would make her pay.

No, Miranda Steele, it won't be long. Soon I'll have you right where you belong.

Completely at my mercy.

THE END

ABOUT THE AUTHOR

Linsey Lanier writes chilling mystery-thrillers that keep you up at night.

Daughter of a WWII Navy Lieutenant, she has written fiction for more than fifteen years. She has authored over two dozen novels and short stories, including the popular Miranda's Rights Mystery series and the Miranda and Parker Mystery series. Someone Else's Daughter has received over 1,000 reviews and more than 500,000 downloads.

Linsey is a member of International Thriller Writers, Private Eye Writers of America, and Romance Writers of America, the Kiss of Death chapter. Her books have been nominated in several RWA-sponsored contests.

In her spare time, Linsey enjoys watching crime shows with her husband of over two decades and trying to figure out "who-dun-it." But her favorite activity is writing and creating entertaining new stories for her readers.

She's always working on a new book, currently books in the Miranda and Parker Mystery series (a continuation of the Miranda's Rights Mystery series). For alerts on her latest releases join Linsey's mailing list at linseylanier.com

For more of Linsey's books, visit her website at **www.linseylanier.com**

Proofreaad by

Donna Rich